The Sunrise Cove Inn

The Vineyard Sunset Series

Katie Winters

Chapter One

Hotheaded. Quick-witted. Stunningly beautiful. "The kind of woman who always gets what she wants."

He had always said these things with a wink. Always with a note of love and excitement.

Until all that had disappeared in the blink of an eye.

Susan laughed at herself. But it was true. She had loved hearing what she looked like through his eyes. In the beginning, she was a bright-eyed and glowing eighteen-year-old girl with aspirations to be a criminal lawyer and eventually take on the world. Richard had been the same—arrogant and sure of himself—but that had suited her just fine. Together, she had known that nothing could take them down.

That was nothing except the spunky little thirty-one-year-old secretary named Penelope.

"What a cliché," Susan muttered to herself. She stood for the last time in her law office and scanned the room. At forty-four years old, she was one of two partners in the law offices of Harris and Harris. This had been her entire career. She and Richard had fought and struggled, given their time and energy and nearly everything else to this business.

Now, the business had chewed up her marriage and spit her out. Their divorce had been finalized six months before. This had given Susan enough time to finish the rest of her cases, explain the situation to her children, and pack up her box of things.

Her husband planned to buy her out. What would it be then, she wondered. The law offices of... Just One Harris? Cheating Harris? The Leftover Harris? She laughed to herself. She wished she could point the finger at her twentysomething self and say, "Maybe work with someone else."

Oh, but she had been a romantic back then. She couldn't have known.

She clenched her hand into a fist and placed it steadily at the center of the desk. She had sat right there for some eighteen years—since she had passed the bar— and couldn't imagine working anywhere else.

Of course, now, she planned to take a good six months off. It would give her time to regroup and recharge—something she needed desperately. Also, to celebrate her daughter's new engagement—and hang with her two little twin grandchildren.

There was other stuff to deal with, bigger issues at hand. But she liked to shove those things into the back of her mind and press forward. She had to be stubborn, quick-witted, and hotheaded for herself and only for herself, now, and never again for him.

Susan slipped the top on her box of things and walked toward the hall. When she reached it, she heard the shrill voice of Penelope and the corresponding laughter from her ex-husband. That laugh sounded a little bit different than it used to. It used to be genuine, open, and fill her with light. Now, it wrapped itself around her neck and made it difficult for her to breathe.

She had told Richard she would be at the office to pick up her things that evening. She had told him so that he would keep his distance. They still remained at the same house together—with her taking over the apartment they had built for Richard's mother before she had passed away. Despite their close living quarters, they hadn't seen each other in several weeks. At least, not up close.

Penelope and Richard stumbled around the corner and stopped short as they stared at her like deer in headlights. Susan arched her brow angrily. Richard's assured smile fell off his lips and onto the floor. Beside him, Penelope gave a weird giggle. She had recently quit her job as his secretary because he had given her the cash to go back to college.

At least, that was the gossip Susan had heard. She hadn't bothered to ask Richard about it.

Richard smeared his hand across the back of his head. There was just the beginning of a bald spot under his still-jet-black hair. He looked thin and powerful, much better in the suit she didn't recognize than he had in years. Probably, he and Penelope worked out together. That was the kind of thing younger couples did—and these days, Richard was nothing but a wannabe younger man. In the middle of a midlife crisis, she thought to herself.

"I just came to get the rest of my things from my office," Susan said. She didn't give him any kind of smile. He didn't deserve it.

"Right. You had said that. I forgot," Richard replied. His voice was gravelly and dark, almost dangerous. She remembered when he had talked to criminals like that in their first few years as lawyers for Harris and Harris. His eyes had flickered dangerously.

Now, she was the danger. The final block in the road between him and his happiness.

But she was on her way out.

"Excuse me," Susan said. She shot forward and cut between Penelope and Richard. Penelope hopped to the side, her ankle crumpling a bit as she went. She had always worn six-inch heels, and today was no different.

"Don't let your husband hire a hot secretary," her friends told her repeatedly.

"But I trust him. We're professionals. We're criminal lawyers, for goodness' sake. Richard knows there are more meaningful things in life. He respects his family. He respects me."

When she reached the elevator, Richard called for her. "Susan, you're going to get the last of your stuff out tonight, right?"

She whipped around, her nostrils flared. Her dark brunette hair wafted down her shoulders. "We have a few more things to discuss before I leave."

Penelope looked anxious. To be honest, Susan enjoyed the strange expression she wore. She looked like a child stuck in the middle of an adult conversation.

"But I wouldn't want to keep you now for that discussion," Susan said brightly. "I know you have much better things to do than to talk about the good old days with your ex-wife."

The words were obviously cutting. They held the kind of emotion behind them that she'd always used while working as a lawyer beside him. Her friends had laughed about this many times when she had told them. *"Imagine two lawyers getting divorced. You'll destroy each other with all the games you'll play."*

Truthfully, though, Susan didn't want anything to do with all these strange and sinister games. It had been a moment of weakness. That was all.

Outside, she inhaled the late-May, summery air and gripped the edge of her Prius to steady herself. Just a few parking spots away sat Richard's newly purchased Lamborghini. He didn't care about the destruction of the environment or anyone else but himself, for that matter.

The streets of Newark, New Jersey, were congested. Dropping her head against her car seat, Susan listened as the radio crackled from weather to a '90s song she had loved, then back to an interview with a Green Party candidate. She glanced at her fingers on the steering wheel, which were bare and void of rings. Taking them off had been a huge weight off her chest—freedom from the man who couldn't love her anymore. Wasn't that enough?

They had bought the massive house in Newark when their business had boomed, and they had invested in a few key companies. It had six bedrooms, a small indoor pool, a downstairs bar area where they'd always played board games as a family, and a gorgeous garden in the back. Susan had liked to keep the garden up herself at first but had soon passed that off to a gardener when she'd had too many cases to go over. There was never enough time in the day. She parked her Prius in the back, with its private entrance to the apartment attached to the main house. As she headed toward the door, she stopped to gaze at the gorgeous rose bush that had, strangely enough, decided to bloom a tiny bit early. They'd already had plenty of warm days, and its bright red petals had sprung forth. For whatever reason, the sight of this filled her with a sense of earnestness.

Deep in her heart, she felt it was time for her to go.

The apartment still held the same furniture from when Richard's mother lived there. It had been a tiny passion project for Susan and her daughter, Amanda, when she had been twelve or thirteen. Susan loved remembering those days; both stretched out over magazines, analyzing paint colors and wallpaper designs. Amanda now wanted to be a lawyer like her parents, which thrilled Susan, although she had always sensed that Amanda had an inner artist in her, as well.

She had added photos of her children to the apartment—photos she had taken from the main house since she guessed her husband didn't pause and reflect so often. There she was, beautiful twenty-two-year-old Amanda. Everyone remarked that she looked just like Susan—but in reality, Susan thought Amanda looked a lot more like her mother, Anna. Amanda's fiancé, Chris Mirren, couldn't have been a better fit for her. Susan already had countless ideas about how to decorate and cater to the wedding. After Amanda told her about her engagement through tears, Amanda said, "I'm sorry. I hope this isn't too hard for you since you and Dad..."

"That's so silly!" Susan had cried. "Your father and I did all we could to stay together." Not true. "It's your time to have the happiness we used to have." Had they really ever? Susan couldn't remember now.

Then, there was her eldest son, Jake. She had placed his picture next to his wife, Kristen, and their fraternal twins, Cody and Samantha, age two, on her desk, next to her closed laptop. Jake was twenty-five years old. Susan had gotten pregnant with him at age nineteen. At forty-four, she now recognized what a baby she had been all those years ago.

She had done what she'd thought was right: she had dropped out of college, had Jake, and then given birth to Amanda three years later. She and Richard married when she was only twenty-four, toting two gorgeous and bubbly children along with them. After that, Richard allowed her to return to school, and she graduated with honors. The two of them were going to take on the world together. And they did for a little while.

Every single step of the way, she had assumed she had done the right thing.

Even still, it felt as if her hands were empty. She no longer had her career. She planned to stay with her son, his wife, and her grandchildren for a few weeks until she could fully decide what to do next.

All those years since she had left Martha's Vineyard. She had been a fresh-faced eighteen-year-old, with nothing to lose and a huge, gut-wrenching desire to get off that island and see the rest of the world.

Now, she had everything to lose—and she felt that she really had.

Susan placed a frozen burrito in the microwave. In earlier times, she would always have dinner ready (or brought home takeout) for the children at seven sharp. Now, she did what she had to do to keep herself alive.

Her phone buzzed from the counter, jarring her from her thoughts. When she had practiced as a lawyer, that thing had buzzed nonstop—so much so that it had given her an anxiety disorder for a few years. What was it the Dr. had said recently about that? All that cortisol in your system over the years couldn't have helped. Great. She had stressed herself to bad health.

The phone call was from her aunt Kerry. Susan hadn't heard from Aunt Kerry outside of random Christmas cards in many, many years. She balked at it as if it was a message from another time. After seven rings, realizing she wasn't going to hang up, Susan grabbed it and stabbed the talk button.

"Hello?" she answered, almost sounding breathless, like a woman who'd just been left by her husband for his secretary.

"Susan? Is that you?"

The voice wasn't welcoming. It sounded rattled and rushed.

"Yes, Aunt Kerry. Are you okay? Is something wrong?"

"Yes, darling. I'm fine. But your father isn't. He's in the hospital, honey, and you need to get here as soon as possible. Do you understand me?"

Chapter Two

Susan was good under pressure. She always supposed this was tied up in all the chaos of her teenage years. She had been the eldest daughter of three sisters, the one who'd had to take charge after everything had happened. As soon as she'd been able to, she had immediately moved away, had a baby, and then things had taken off for her after that. And she had never cracked.

This call from Aunt Kerry was no different.

She heard herself respond calmly. "I'll get there as soon as I can. Thank you for calling, Aunt Kerry. Yes, I look forward to seeing you too."

During her final words, she heard the back door open and clip shut. The familiar footsteps of her daughter Amanda grew louder. Finally, Amanda appeared in the doorway to the kitchen, her hands on her hips and her brow furrowed. Again, Susan felt that jolt of recognition. She was the spitting image of her beautiful mother, Anna. Anna. Dead at thirty-eight.

"What was that about?" Amanda asked, leaning against the doorjamb.

"Aunt Kerry called. Apparently, Dad's in the hospital," Susan said.

Amanda looked worried, but Susan knew it was only for her sake. Amanda had only met her grandfather once, fifteen years before. She had been only six or seven years old at the time.

"Did she say what's wrong?" She swept toward the fridge and opened it, an old ritual Susan missed from the days when Amanda and Jake lived at home. Back when they'd been a real family.

"They're doing some tests. I don't know," Susan tried to explain. She leaned heavily against the counter. After the drama of seeing Penelope and Richard at the office, packing up her things, and feeling the pressure of leaving the home she had shared with him for the past era of her life—she felt exhausted and mentally drained. Now, there was this to worry about.

"And you're really going to go there?" Amanda sounded doubtful as she slipped the top off a bottle of raspberry-cranberry juice and poured herself a small glass.

Susan hesitated. She had told her aunt Kerry she could come immediately, without a second thought. In her ordinary life, this would have been outside her limits. She'd always had cases to work on, friends to see, Richard and the kids to take care of.

"I just mean, you haven't been back to the Vineyard in like, what, twelve years?" Amanda asked as she took a sip from her glass.

"Fifteen," Susan corrected. "And to tell you the truth,

I don't know. But right now, I've closed my last case. Your father's going to buy my part of the business, and honestly, I don't have anything to stay here for."

"Jake and I take offense to that," Amanda said with a smile. "I just know you planned to take six months for yourself—and this doesn't sound like any kind of vacation, Mom."

"Even if I'm there for just a few days, I think I should go. I would really regret it if something happened," Susan said.

Susan glanced back through the rest of the apartment. She had packed up most of it, except for a few odds and ends that she hadn't had time to slip into boxes.

"Do you have an hour or two to help me with the last of this?" Susan asked. "I just realized that if I'm heading off to Martha's Vineyard, I need to get this done. Maybe I can catch the first ferry tomorrow if I drive to Falmouth tonight."

"It's still crazy that Dad's kicking you out," Amanda said. Her eyes glittered ominously. Since the divorce had been finalized, she had been pretty vocal about her support of her mother. *The secretary? She's not much older than me!* Had been the words she had screamed when she had learned of the real reason for the divorce.

"He's not. I mean, not really. We came to an agreement that suits us both best. Besides, it'll be nice to spend more time with Samantha and Cody. With all the drama, I feel like I missed a lot of their early years."

"How can they be the cutest creatures in the world but also the evilest?" Amanda asked, grinning widely.

It was true that the twins had spent most of their first few months of life screaming as loudly as possible. Jake had joked that they had set new sound records. Susan and Amanda had helped out as much as they could, given that Susan had still practiced criminal law, and Amanda had been smack-dab in the middle of undergrad at the time.

Amanda and Susan got to work packing up the last of the boxes. They had it all packed up in Susan's Prius in less than thirty minutes. She blinked at the key, still attached to her car key ring. Did she feel ready to give it up?

But no. She had to be quick about this. There was no time to swim in her nostalgia—not with her dad in the hospital.

If she had learned anything recently, it was that you never really knew how much time you had left. It was best not to waste it on things that no longer served you.

Susan entered the main house from the back and placed the keys on the marble countertops, which they'd installed maybe five years before. She had drunk countless glasses of French wine at those countertops, poring over criminal documents, clacking her nails across the top in a way that had always irritated Richard. All those hours, when she had just assumed, stupidly, maybe, that this would be her life forever. A life to grow old next to someone.

She realized something in the kitchen: this was no longer her house. Although it was still suited up with the appliances she had picked, the wall color she had chosen, she knew the refrigerator was stocked with food she hadn't bought. Even the air had a different smell to it. A perfume she had never worn. A sign that Richard and the house had moved on without her.

"Goodbye," she murmured to the house "You were

good to me. Maybe hold back just a tiny bit for the next round."

Amanda followed Susan in her little Chevy for the fifteen-minute drive to her son Jake's house. Jake worked as an engineer and made a hefty salary, despite his age of twenty-five. Susan was mesmerized by his incredible way with numbers. He had always been a bit more reserved and cerebral, something his wife, Kristen, laughed about since she was always such an extrovert. Still, their relationship balanced itself out really well. They were truly the perfect couple.

Jake was the spitting image of his dad at that age. He popped out of the garage and gave Amanda and Susan a wave as he tossed the last of a chip into his mouth and chewed. When Susan got out of the car, he hugged her and said, "We're so glad to have you here. You can stay however long you want."

But Amanda interjected before Susan had the chance to explain. "Mom's going to Martha's Vineyard."

Jake's blue eyes bugged out. "What?"

Susan felt put on the spot. "Your grandfather is in the hospital. If I hurry, I can make it on the first ferry tomorrow. I just have to get to Falmouth tonight."

"Grandpa Wes. Oh." Jake formed the words as if they were in a foreign language. Just like Amanda, his only real memories of his grandfather were Susan's stories.

He was mean. Sometimes, a drinker. A workaholic.

He had ruined her life. He'd ruined her sisters' lives.

And she had never forgiven him for any of it.

The thought struck her then like a smack across the cheek. She forced the thought away and smiled at her children as they opened the trunk of her Prius and helped her carry the boxes into the spare area of the house, which

Kristen and Jake had reserved for her. Susan assumed she would be back in a few days, maybe a week at most, depending on the situation she was about to embark on.

Once they dropped off her things, Susan packed herself a suitcase and reappeared in the kitchen. Samantha and Cody sat up in their high chairs with little bibs across their chests. Samantha cooed and lifted her arms. "Grandma!" Cody smacked his plastic spoon against the high chair excitedly.

"Are you sure you don't want to wait and leave tomorrow, Mom?" Jake asked from the stove. He stirred some pasta, an act she had never in her life seen Richard perform.

She'd at least done one thing right. Her son knew how to do household tasks.

"Aunt Kerry was really specific about coming as fast as I could. Besides, you know me. I wouldn't be able to sleep tonight if I stayed," Susan said. She dotted a kiss on Samantha's and Cody's foreheads and chuckled at their clownish reactions. "Is Kristen still at the school?"

"Yeah. She's still coaching girls' tennis. She'll be home in a bit, but I guess she'll miss you."

"Give her my love, honey," Susan said. She kissed her son on the cheek, then turned to hug Amanda goodbye. As she did, she remembered. "Shoot! You start your internship tomorrow, don't you? I completely forgot."

Amanda nodded. She had taken up an internship at a nearby firm in a criminal law department. At twenty-two, she would start law school that fall. Where was the time going?

"Call me after. I want to hear all about it," Susan said, pointing at her daughter.

"I haven't even been to law school yet. They'll probably just make me do paperwork," Amanda said with a laugh.

"Doing paperwork is seventy percent of every job in the world. I would have gone nuts without all that help from interns. You're much more important than you know."

Back in her Prius, her heart shifted and beat harder, louder. She checked the ferry times on her phone, shoving her thoughts into the tiny recesses in the back of her mind. She kept a lot of things tucked away back there.

Things she didn't want her children to know.

Things she didn't want to face herself.

"Secretive." This had been a way Richard had described her too. Yet, in the end, it had been his secrets that had destroyed their marriage.

But there had always been things about Susan that Richard didn't know.

She had preferred it that way. *"You have to keep a bit of yourself for yourself,"* she had told a girlfriend a long time ago.

It was still early evening. This would give Susan enough time to reach Falmouth and fall immediately into an inn bed. She cranked the engine as another few texts buzzed through her phone.

> Richard: Thanks for getting your stuff out. Sorry for the run-in today. I got my hours mixed up. Scheduling was always your strong suit, not mine. Take care.

For a second, Susan contemplated telling Richard what she was about to do. Go to Martha's Vineyard. See her father again for the first time in fifteen years. Face whatever was left of her past.

But Richard wasn't a part of her life anymore. He was nothing to her now.

And she didn't want to keep thinking about him.

She eased her Prius back down the driveway. She had a ferry to catch.

Chapter Three

Susan couldn't remember the last time she had checked into an inn without her husband. She gave a little "hurrah" for this moment as she passed her credit card over the counter and gave the concierge a sleepy smile. She had driven nonstop for the past five-some hours, and all she wanted to do was crash between some high-count bed sheets.

Upstairs, though, she really couldn't sleep. She donned a nightgown, washed her face, and smeared on various night creams. Then, she took to pacing, just as she had done during the days when she'd had particularly rough cases to deal with.

She hadn't been to Falmouth in fifteen years, not since she had left the Vineyard in a huge huff. Susan had been twenty-nine, with two young children, and had had this stupid itch to head out to where she had grown up, make peace with her father, and show her kids some of her favorite sights.

At the time, she thought, *I'm an adult. I have two chil-*

dren of my own. I can see through everything my father's done and forgive him.

But it hadn't taken long for them to leap back into their long-standing disputes. She remembered screaming at him outside the Sunrise Cove Inn, her children just behind her. "That's the thing about you, Dad. You're just like this island. You'll never change. You're stuck back in time, and you can't see it. You can't see how selfish and arrogant you are."

She couldn't even fully remember what had started the fight.

She guessed she just couldn't forgive him for what he had done all those years ago.

She would never forget it.

After that, Susan hadn't heard from her dad for a few years. She had told Richard at the time that she didn't care if she ever spoke to him again. Some years, he remembered her kids' birthdays and sent cards and money. Other years, there was nothing but silence.

She wondered what her dad would think when he saw her at the hospital. Probably calling her to the Vine-yard hadn't been his idea. Aunt Kerry had always been like that: meddling in a sweet way. She certainly never meant any harm and only had her brother's interests at heart.

Regardless, it was true what Susan had told Amanda. She didn't have anything to stay in Newark for at the moment.

The first ferry of the morning left at eight. Goose bumps popped up and down Susan's arms and legs as she parked her Prius in long-term parking and then purchased a ticket at the ticket stand. The woman who passed the ticket to her and said a chipper, "Have a great day on the

Vineyard!" could have been any other woman she'd ever seen sell tickets at that very stand. It was as if time had stopped. Upstairs in the café, she bought herself a large coffee and a bran muffin, which she hardly touched as she gazed out at the glittering water. It was still early in the season, which meant the boat was only about half full. Tourists flocked to the Vineyard in June, July, and August, so much so that the normal population of 15,000 people skyrocketed to close to 100,000.

Susan had always loved this about the island. It was always morphing, shifting, and becoming something more beautiful and alive. And then, just at the breaking point, it closed up shop. Autumn would come, and with it another season, a softer and more peaceful one. All the hotel and inn and restaurant owners, the owners of tour companies, and whale-watching boats would come together in friendship and camaraderie to celebrate the closing of the summer season. Although Susan's family had always been tight-knit on the Vineyard—both of her parents had grown up there, and most of their siblings hadn't left—and they also had dear friends who felt like family.

Memories flooded through her. It was difficult to breathe as she thought about fishing on the Nantucket Sound, whale watching, and kissing boys at Felix Neck. She had always helped her mother with responsibilities at the inn and laughed with her. She and her friends always loved to go hiking and swimming; they'd built bonfires and danced, beneath the moon while catching fireflies.

Yes, growing up on the Vineyard had been almost picture-perfect.

Until it hadn't been any more.

She caught sight of the Vineyard for the first time a few minutes later. She could feel herself in so many other forms:

19

twenty-nine, trying to keep track of Jake and Amanda and all their toys and crayons; eighteen years old and escaping the island, telling anyone who would listen that she was never coming back; all the years before that, too, as a wild-eyed teenager, in love with everything and everyone, but also a responsible and loving older sister, a girl who had pledged to do anything for her younger sisters.

Christine. Lola.

It had been so many years since she had even heard their voices.

They didn't know she had gotten divorced.

They didn't know about anything.

Suddenly, Susan felt more alone than she had ever felt. Ironic, really, since this was the opposite feeling you were supposed to feel when arriving at the home where you grew up.

Aunt Kerry had texted her that morning to say that her husband, Uncle Trevor, would be at the dock to pick her up and drive her to the hospital. Susan had always loved her uncle Trevor. Aunt Kerry was her father's older sister, and Uncle Trevor had always been her sturdy, loving, and stoic husband, handsome with jet-black hair, thick eyebrows, and a broad chest. They had four children, Steven, Kelli, Charlotte, and Claire—all of whom, as far as Susan knew, had remained on the island.

Susan stepped off the ferry on quivering legs. She felt she had walked directly into her past, updated only with the new fashions. Around her, tourists flocked from the boat and onto the Vineyard at the port at Oak Bluffs. Couples latched their hands together excitedly, beaming at each other, while Susan wished she could tell her heart to feel something besides dread.

At the edge of the dock, she entered the parking area and slowly scanned it, hunting for Uncle Trevor. Suddenly, a massive hand sprang up from the side of a truck and whipped back and forth. Her eyes caught the face attached to that hand: stoic, handsome, despite his seventy-one years, with salt-and-pepper hair that had still resisted thinning.

Susan walked up to the truck and placed her hands on her hips. Her eyes connected with his as she shook her head.

"My goodness. You're a sight for sore eyes," she said, smiling at her uncle. He was still as handsome as ever.

Uncle Trevor let out his good-natured laugh. He cut out from the side of the truck, admittedly a bit slower than he had fifteen years before, and wrapped her in a massive bear hug. If anything, this was the punch to the heart Susan had been waiting for. She could feel the lump in her throat but swallowed to keep it at bay.

I'm back. I'm here. This is where I used to belong.

"Susan! It is so terrific to see you," Uncle Trevor said. He beamed at her as the hug broke. "And looking prettier than ever. Your cousins are dying to see you. It's been... how long? Oh, shoot, I don't care. Let's get you up to the hospital."

Susan let her much-older uncle take her suitcase and fling it into the back seat of the double-wide truck. She then slid into the passenger seat.

"Must be strange to be back here," Uncle Trevor said. He turned quickly to gaze out the back window as the truck eased through the traffic and pedestrians. "I've never spent more than a week off the island. And you— you've now spent most of your life off of it!"

"I guess you're right," Susan said. "I hadn't thought about it that way."

"Oh, my kids love to brag about you," Uncle Trevor continued. He cut the truck into drive and slowly skated through the rest of the parking lot. "They love to talk about their big-deal criminal lawyer cousin in Newark. Tell you the truth; I think one or two of 'em wish they would have spent a bit more time off the island like you and your sisters. By the way. How are they doing? Christine? Lola?"

Susan swallowed. She had to lie; she couldn't enter into this world of family and kinship with, *I haven't spoken to my sisters in years.* So, she said, "They're pretty good."

"They must feel pretty crazy about your dad. I'll let Aunt Kerry tell you more when we get there. She's been, well. She's been out of her mind. I'm just glad to have you here."

Should Susan have told her sisters about their dad? She supposed she should have, although it struck her that it hadn't even occurred to her until just then.

What had happened to her family?

The drive to the hospital in Oak Bluffs only took about five minutes longer due to traffic. It was still early in the morning, but everywhere they turned, it seemed there were horses and carriages, people jutting out into traffic excitedly, everyone big-eyed with wonder. Uncle Trevor clucked his tongue. "I guess it's getting to about that time, isn't it?"

"They're back," Susan said jokingly. Tourists had always been their bread and butter—but it was fun to be annoyed with them too. You had to in that business. At least, that was what her mother had always said.

Her uncle and aunt were now retired, but they'd made their money through the real estate on the Vineyard —mostly selling vacation homes to very rich buyers. This had suited them handsomely. They had always made a great team—Uncle Trevor's more trusting nature and Aunt Kerry's upbeat chatter and neighborly feel. She had baked a lot of cookies and sold a lot of houses. And when tourists grew bored with their enormous, expensive vacation homes, they always hired Uncle Trevor and Aunt Kerry to sell them to the next ones lined up.

When they reached the hospital, Susan had another out-of-body moment. Again, she glanced at her uncle as he hurriedly unbuckled his seat belt and gestured with his head. "Come on. She's waiting for us."

Susan slipped out of the truck and followed her uncle Trevor slowly toward the hospital's glass doors. This was a nightmare come to life.

Time had caught up to her. And she couldn't avoid it any longer.

Chapter Four

Aunt Kerry smelled the same, like lavender and sea salt and something else, maybe her cooking. Susan remembered she had always been the best cook. Aunt Kerry wrapped her arms around her, dropped her head against Susan's shoulder, and let out, "She's back. Oh, my darling girl is back."

Like Uncle Trevor, Aunt Kerry had aged gracefully. When she eased back, Susan studied her face for a second: the glittering green eyes, the now-white yet very smooth and beautiful bob, the thin cheeks, and the regal-looking nose. She wore white slacks and a light blue sweater set, and she gripped Susan's shoulders hard, proof that her inner strength had never faded.

"It's good to see you, Aunt Kerry," Susan said. Her heart swelled. Now that she was standing in front of her aunt, she realized how much she had missed her.

"I'm so glad you came! I don't know quite what to do with him," Aunt Kerry said. She dropped her hand and grabbed her handkerchief to dab at the side of her eye. "It's been a rather difficult six months. And now..."

Susan felt like she had just flipped midway through a book without bothering to read the beginning. What did she mean? A difficult six months?

"What happened, Aunt Kerry?" she asked, her brow furrowed. She had never seen this strong-as-a-rock woman break down like this before.

"I heard the sirens in the distance, but I didn't think anything of it," Aunt Kerry explained. She sounded flabbergasted as if she wasn't sure where to start the story. "You know, it seems like the tourists are always getting themselves into trouble."

"Sirens?" Susan's heart rattled around in her chest.

"Yes. Your father was cooking. He left the stove for a few moments—it's a really old stove, you must remember that—and something caught on fire. He's a quick old man, that's for certain, and he hustled to the kitchen and tried to put it out. He succeeded, but not without some hefty second-degree burns."

"Oh my god," Susan whispered. "This all happened yesterday?"

"The doctor knows us, of course, and called me right away," Aunt Kerry continued.

Still, it didn't make sense that they'd kept him overnight for a second-degree burn. Susan arched her brow and considered possible questions. Something hovered in the air between her and Aunt Kerry. As a secret-keeper herself, she was good at sniffing out other people.

"Do you want to see him?" Aunt Kerry asked.

Susan hesitated, but Aunt Kerry placed her hand on her lower back and coaxed her toward the hospital room her father occupied. "He doesn't know you're coming. I hope you don't give him a heart attack."

"Ha." Susan wasn't really in the mood for jokes.

Her father—the great Wesley Sheridan, longtime owner of Sunrise Cove Inn and father of three Sheridan sisters, sat upright in his hospital bed with his gaze cast toward the window. He was a great lover of nature—of air, water, fishing, and sailing—and had always considered many hours inside to be a complete waste, regardless of the season. He still had dark hair, although it was peppered with white, and he looked as if he had lost a little muscle. His arm was wrapped tight in bandages, proof of what had happened the day before.

Aunt Kerry clucked her tongue. "Wes? Don't you want to see who came for a visit?"

Wes Sheridan turned his head slowly. His eyes met Susan's, and suddenly, a look of complete and powerful love washed over him. Susan's heart broke into a million pieces. She couldn't say a thing as the lump in her throat now threatened to choke her.

All those years away from the Vineyard. All those conversations they'd never had. All those fights they had lingered on—and for what?

Suddenly, she felt overwhelmed.

Why had she hated him so much?

He was alone in the world, and now so was she.

She couldn't take it. She stepped toward him and fell into a hug. Her head found his shoulder and burrowed there. It was as if she was seven years old again and going to her dad for comfort. It was as if time didn't matter anymore. If she closed her eyes tight enough, she could imagine her mother in the kitchen, baking bread, her sisters upstairs, playing house. Her father, home after a long day at the inn, hugging her tight. Those were her happy memories.

When the hug broke, Susan tried on a smile. Finally, she said, "You were never that good at cooking, Dad, but this really takes the cake."

"You know how much I love a bit of drama," her dad said with a laugh.

"Maybe keep it to first-degree burns next time. It's just as much of a story without all the pain."

"I'll keep that in mind," Wes said. He smiled wider, and his eyes kept up that twinkle. "Susan Sheridan. You know, I'd recognize you anywhere. You sure are a stunner, just like your mother used to be. Just gorgeous."

Susan rolled her eyes but secretly loved that he had used her maiden name. She had considered taking it back now that the divorce was finalized. She wanted to shake off the last of Richard.

Her dad found her hand. "I hope your babies are doing okay. Amanda and Jake."

"Not babies anymore, sadly," Susan said, flashing him a soft smile. "You never told me how painful that would be."

"No. Nobody can prepare you for that. Not even your old dad."

Again, Susan felt her heart blast into several pieces. She swallowed and tried to keep her lips turned up into a smile. As she tried to think of something else to say, the doctor entered behind her and cleared his throat.

"Susan Sheridan! Good to see you again," he said in a deep baritone voice.

Susan turned to find Dr. Thomas Miller, a guy she'd gone to high school with. If her memory was correct, he had left the island for several years to go to medical school at Harvard before returning to the Vineyard. He looked almost the same, although he had lost a good bit of hair on top.

"Tommy, hey," she said. "Good to see you too."

"I see you've found our new ward," he said. "Truth be told, we don't have to keep him here much longer."

"That's good to hear," Susan said as she stole another glance at her father.

"I would like to talk to you privately for a few minutes, though, if you have the time," Dr. Miller said. His eyes found Aunt Kerry's, as well. "Both of you."

Susan and Aunt Kerry followed Dr. Miller into a separate office down the hall. Susan was overwhelmed but kept her cool, grateful for her lawyer ways. When they reached the office, they sat in front of Dr. Miller, who clasped his hands and said, in a matter-of-fact way, "I think it's good we kept him overnight. He was in the middle of another confused spell, and I don't know what would have happened if we had let him go home last night like he wanted."

Aunt Kerry gave a wry laugh. "He always wants to go home. He doesn't trust doctors."

"I know. After all these months of working with him, that's become pretty clear," Dr. Miller said.

Susan furrowed her brow. "I'm sorry. What do you mean about confusing spells?"

Dr. Miller glanced toward Aunt Kerry. He looked as if he had just spilled something. "I'm sorry. I thought you'd been told, Susan."

Aunt Kerry shifted her weight and crossed her legs swiftly, ever a lady. "Susan, please don't be angry with me. You were hours away, and you haven't exactly been on speaking terms with your father in, what, fifteen years?"

Susan's jaw dropped. Dr. Miller stared directly at the blank paper on his desk as the tension filled the room.

"He has dementia," Aunt Kerry said. "We started to notice the signs about a year ago, I guess. Just little things. He forgot things he always remembered."

"And this was why he burned himself. He forgot he had the stove on," Susan muttered.

"That's what we assume. It's not like him to forget something like that. Not like the old him, anyway," Aunt Kerry said as she looked at her hands resting in her lap.

"You should have called me right away," Susan said.

Aunt Kerry gave a sad shrug. "You're here now. That's all that matters."

This shut Susan up for a long time. And in truth, with all the chaos in her own life—the divorce, among other things—it wasn't as if she would have been in the best position to come out here a year ago or even six months ago. Still, she was angry that she hadn't been told sooner. All she wanted to do was be there for them now. Especially now that she'd seen her father and felt the built-up anger toward him melt away. It was as if it had all been in her imagination.

Time healed all wounds. It had been an expression her mother had said often, especially when it came down to Susan and her sisters' little fights. Within hours, they always made up. It was just what they did.

Susan listened as Dr. Miller described the current state of her father's brain, the trajectory of dementia, and what he assumed would happen next.

"He's going to have more and more of these spells going forward, I'm afraid," Dr. Miller said. "It's no longer safe to keep him in that big house alone. He could have burned down the whole house. He could have really hurt himself. The fact that he got out of this okay is a blessing. But it's time to take action before it's too late."

Aunt Kerry and Susan thanked Dr. Miller. He admitted that he had to head out to see other patients and that her father was free to go whenever they were ready to take him. "But remember. Don't leave him alone. Even if he thinks he's okay, his mental state is a slippery slope. One minute, he'll be fine—and the next, he might not remember where he is or even who he is."

In the hallway, Susan and Aunt Kerry stood for a long time without speaking. Susan felt her lawyer nature spike up. She wanted to blare her anger again at her aunt Kerry. But in truth, she knew that the anger was more for herself. She hated how much she had missed. She hated that she had become just another piece of the past.

Chapter Five

"I'm sorry about what I said in there," Aunt Kerry said. She kept her chin upright and her eyes straight ahead. She wasn't the sort of woman to grovel. "You have to understand how it felt from our perspective. We felt you were long gone."

Susan swallowed. "I understand." She had to. There was no way to move forward except through apologies and acceptance. These people had been there at the very beginning of her life. Now, they needed her more than anything.

"I know I've missed so much," Susan continued.

Aunt Kerry gave a slight laugh. "Not so much, really. You know how it is on the island. Time has its own way. But indeed, it has marched on without you. Now, you have that big career in Newark. You must seldom think about us here in the Vineyard. And why would you? When you were eighteen, you were such a determined little thing. I didn't know what to do with any of you—not with you, Christine, or Lola."

Susan knew that she meant during the time after their

mother's death. The words stung. Aunt Kerry and her mother had never been very close—and Susan had always suspected it was because her dad had told Aunt Kerry lies about her mother. Lies that created a distance between them. Of course, they'd never allowed it to impact her personal relationship with her aunt, uncle, and cousins.

Susan followed Aunt Kerry back down the hall. She felt speechless. But there was a fire in her belly, energy that she hadn't felt for a long time. She knew what she had to do. Her life was finished back in Newark. Her job was finished; she'd moved out of the house she had loved; she planned to live on with her son, his wife, and their twins—but what kind of happiness remained for her there? She imagined herself growing old there: not as herself, but as the twins' grandmother. She was only forty-four years old. Didn't she have time to build something else?

And wasn't Martha's Vineyard a good place to start?

They reached her father's hospital room again. The nurse had given him back his street clothes, and he sat at the edge of the bed in a button-up blue-and-white-plaid shirt and a pair of jeans. His large hands were placed steadily on his lap, and he stared straight ahead as if he were waiting for something. When Susan entered through the door, she had the sudden and horrible suspicion that he would forget who she was—that they would have to go through the whole rigmarole of her coming back into his life again.

Luckily, dementia hadn't blotted her out—yet. The doctor had explained that it was still in its early stages.

"There she is. My beautiful daughter." Wes beamed at her.

"I see they're kicking you out of here," Susan said and

chuckled. She had forgotten that she and her dad had had this kind of light banter throughout her early life and even into her teenage years. She had forgotten that when they hadn't been fighting, they'd been laughing.

"I begged 'em to let me stay, but they thought I might try to burn this place down too," Wes returned with a wink.

"Let's bring this arsonist back home," Susan said. "As bad as a teenager, I swear."

"Your teenagers aren't any trouble, are they?" her father asked. He stood evenly, wincing just a tiny bit as he put all his weight on both feet.

"Not teenagers anymore." Susan felt a strange pang as they returned back to this subject. There would be a lot of this back-and-forth.

A shadow passed over her dad's face. She regretted telling him this—as if she should have made something up, said Amanda still played soccer on the JV team, and Jake was captain of the chess team. But nope. That was another Susan's reality. Not hers.

"Do you have pictures?" her dad asked.

Aunt Kerry stepped outside for a second to talk to Uncle Trevor. Susan searched through her purse for her phone. She swiped for a second to find photos of Jake and Kristen, Cody and Samantha, Amanda and her fiancé, Chris. These were the people she loved the most in the world, the clan she had created for herself when she had abandoned the Vineyard.

Her father studied the photos thoughtfully as she explained who each person was. "How cute are they!" he exclaimed at the sight of his twin great-grandchildren. "Imagine me. A great-grandfather. I never thought I'd make it this long."

"They're adorable," Susan admitted. "So far, their only real talent is screaming."

"Ha. Then they have something in common with my daughters," Wes said, flashing her a grin. "Especially Lola. She cried and cried to high heaven."

"Now that you mention it, I kind of remember that," Susan said as they laughed at the memory.

"You're five years older than she is. I guess that makes sense. Always such a wannabe mama you were. Helping your mother with Lola, giving her a bottle, and even mashing up her baby food for her." Her father's eyes grew misty. "We used to joke that you were twenty-five years old by the time you hit seven."

"Maybe that means I'm into my sixties already," Susan replied with a smile.

Her dad winced. "Gosh. Time really went by, didn't it?"

Susan wasn't ready to get into it. She didn't want to apologize yet—and didn't want to hear his apologies, either. This was her way: action first. Thoughts later. And right now, she was in the middle of a decision that would change the next many months and potentially years of her life.

She had to be sure of it before she said anything.

Aunt Kerry and Uncle Trevor reappeared in the hospital room. "You ready to go, old man?" Uncle Trevor said.

"Who are you calling an old man?" Wes asked. His eyes glittered as he stepped toward the door.

Susan half reached out, wanting to make sure he made it. But he was and had always been too proud to ask for that kind of help. He'd already allowed people to help him when it counted, like with remodeling parts of their family house or parts of the inn.

The Sunrise Cove Inn had been passed down to Wes Sheridan from his parents decades ago when Wes had been thirty-one years old. Anna had been twenty-nine at the time. Before that, both of Susan's parents had worked at the inn. Wes had been a manager, usually spending long nights at the inn when Susan had been small. Back then, she had begged her dad to let her stay up with him while he worked the counter at Sunrise Cove. She loved to feel the inn close down around her—all those people asleep in their separate rooms, telling secrets or staring longingly into the night. She hadn't known what a sucker she'd been for secrets back then.

At thirty-one, Wes had already lost both of his parents and had been faced with a difficult yet worthy future of running the Sunrise Cove Inn. Raise three daughters. Honor his pledge to his wife. In retrospect, it was a lot for a man of thirty-one to tackle. That was only six years older than her Jake was right now. She couldn't imagine him speaking to a crowd of fifteen, let alone managing an entire inn at peak Martha's Vineyard tourist season.

Uncle Trevor decided to take the route that would snake them past the Sunrise Cove Inn so that Susan could see it for the first time in many, many years. She sat in the back of the truck and placed her hand on the glass as they whisked by. The Sunrise Cove Inn could hold around thirty guests, give or take, and had been built in 1940 by her great-grandparents. It had that old-world charm—as though ghosts lurked through the halls. In the past, her dad had kept the white paint on the exterior in top shape. Now, her heart sank to see that the paint was a bit gray and chipped; the green shutters outside the windows were crooked or missing; even the sign that hung out front with the words SUNRISE COVE was rusted and about to fall to the grass below.

"Do you know what that inn means to me? Do you know how important it is? My parents left it to me. They put their heart and soul into it, and my grandparents did it before them. I can't let it die," her father had said over and over again when she had been seventeen, and her mother had just died. Everything had been falling apart around them. What had she begged him for? A little time off? Time to think and try to patch their family back together?

But it had been too late. He could feel the anger from his daughters. He'd probably known that he couldn't rectify the situation.

He'd probably known that they would all run as fast as they could away from him.

The house Susan, Christine, and Lola had grown up in was a ten-minute walk from Sunrise Cove Inn, located at the edge of Oak Bluffs, shrouded by beautiful thick trees and overlooking the water. Like the inn, the house had fallen into its own state of disrepair. It seemed slumped-over, like an architectural version of her own father, and the shutters hung loose. The porch swing that they'd rocked on for hours on end as kids sat lifeless on the porch floor. The lilac color of the paint outside was also chipped. Just looking at it almost brought her to tears, and this hurt Susan's heart. Lilac had been her mother's idea.

She couldn't believe her father had never changed it.

"Let's have some tea. Catch up a bit," Aunt Kerry announced. "Trevor, will you make yourself useful and carry Susan's suitcase?"

Susan felt guilty watching the older man do it. It was

as if they had to uphold these old rules, although so many years had passed. She was just a kid to them; they had to take care of her things for her. She couldn't manage. As she looked around, the nostalgia of salty breezes and fresh-caught seafood raced through her memory. The Vineyard was just off the southern coast of Cape Cod and the ultimate New England summer escape with its gorgeous storybook villages. Susan had so many wonderful memories growing up on the island, but it seemed as though the dark and ugly ones always took grip and would never let go.

Aunt Kerry snaked a key into the front door. Susan remembered with a funny jolt that she had left her house key to this house in the same way she had just left her house key back at Richard's—on the counter, without another word. She had wanted nothing to do with it anymore.

How stupid of her to easily dismiss all this.

Susan walked into the house last. In the foyer, she was struck by the fact that nothing at all had changed since she had last been there. On the right wall hung a picture of her father, her mother, Christine, Lola, and herself, when she'd been about fourteen years old. The photo had been taken while they'd been out on a boat on the Vineyard Sound. She could remember the day so clearly. Lola had spilled orange juice all over her pretty dress and cried for twenty minutes.

She thought about the fact that her dad had dementia, but at least he still remembered the little details like Lola's constant crying.

But there was so much more that had remained the same. Her mother's old chair still sat in the far window of the living area, where the sunlight struck it in this beautiful way most afternoons. She would sit there, drenched in light, with a book on her lap. Sometimes, she read, but other times, she would make up little stories for her daughters. They would sit, captivated beneath her, their legs crossed beneath them.

The chair looked as though it hadn't been sat on in nearly thirty years.

But why? Why had her father kept it?

She couldn't figure it out.

Aunt Kerry went toward the kitchen while Uncle Trevor and her dad sat on the couch, which looked out toward the big bay window, with a view of the water and the forest that cut up from the sand. The kitchen, too, was really similar to how it had been. Even the smell was the same: ginger tea, one of her dad's favorites, and lilacs. She remembered that her mother had asked for a few lilac bushes to be planted just beneath the kitchen window so the kitchen could always smell like lilacs. She walked toward the window and peered down to see the same bushes, their beautiful flowers drifting slightly in the wind.

"How do you take your tea?" Aunt Kerry asked. "Still with a spoonful of sugar?"

Susan laughed. "I forgot I did that. No. I'll just have a little bit of milk, thanks."

"I figured. You have the same trim figure your mother had," Aunt Kerry replied.

"You mean the same one you have. You look amazing, Aunt Kerry. I must know all your secrets," Susan said.

"Oh? When you get old, you don't feel much like eating anymore. What do I care if something tastes good? I've done it all before." She laughed cheerfully. "Besides, my husband eats enough for both of us."

As Aunt Kerry boiled the water, she turned and looked at Susan again. Her eyes swam with emotion. "It must have been a strange thing when you became older than she was."

Susan swallowed the lump in her throat. She knew exactly what Aunt Kerry meant. When she had been thirty-eight years old, the age that her mother had died, she'd felt apprehensive the entire time: as if she had lived past her own expiration date.

"I miss her. I feel her everywhere in this house. I can't understand why he—" Susan began, but she clamped her lips shut. There was so much emotion and drama lurking behind all this. She didn't want to drudge it toward the surface.

Besides, there was so much happening now, so much other stuff to deal with.

Aunt Kerry and Susan carried the teacups to the living area. Uncle Trevor and Wes had struck up a familiar conversation about the various birds they'd seen throughout that spring. They were words Susan had heard so much during her youth that felt so comforting, like waves on the shore. This was home, her home, and she was starting to become angry with herself for staying away for so long.

When Susan and Aunt Kerry sat, there was a strange pause. Susan wished she could pretend that she hadn't been away for as long as she had. It was the elephant in the room.

"I loved seeing the inn again," she said.

Her dad's face brightened. "Oh, yes. That is my pride and joy."

"How has it been there?" Susan asked. She wanted to walk lightly around the subject to see what was actually going on. She couldn't ask anything pointed, like, *why haven't you painted the inn in ten years?* Or *does anyone even check in there anymore?* Things like that.

"Everything's been great," Wes explained. He sounded chipper and sure of himself. "High turnout, all ready for the start of the season. Everyone loves the historical aspect of our little inn. I always tell them that my grandparents built it, and it's been in our family for many decades."

On instinct, Susan turned her eyes toward Aunt Kerry. Kerry looked stricken as if she wanted to interrupt and say something but felt she couldn't. It seemed obvious that things weren't going so well at Sunrise Cove.

But maybe her dad was too proud to say this out loud or share any details.

"I can't wait to go there later." Susan's voice was cultured and upbeat.

"You'll have to see all the old sights," Wes said. "We should take you out on the boat before you have to leave. There's no way Newark is scratching that itch of yours. I know you love the water."

Susan tried to laugh lightheartedly. In truth, it felt as if her entire chest was being squeezed.

Aunt Kerry interrupted. "But you have to know some of the town gossip. My gosh, the Vineyard has been up to its old tricks ever since you left."

"Like what?!"

"Oh, the usual, I suppose. Affairs. Pregnancies."

"Yes. So boring," Susan said sarcastically. "You have to tell me everything."

"Do you ever talk to those dear friends of yours?" Aunt Kerry interjected. "What were their names again?"

"Ah. Lily and Sarah," Susan answered with a smile.

She could picture their beautiful faces so clearly at age eighteen. Recently, they'd added her on social media, which had given her a clearer picture of their current selves. Still, she had found it really hard to reach out. It had just seemed like a different part of her at the time.

"Yep! Those were the girls. So kind. And that high school sweetheart of yours! I see him around. He still brings supplies to the inn," Aunt Kerry said and winked at Susan.

A shudder rollicked through Susan's entire body.

"Scott Frampton?"

"That's him. Yep. He and his brother Chuck took over Frampton Freights from their father," Aunt Kerry replied.

Susan blinked down at her tea, which she had still forgotten to drink. Scott Frampton. She hadn't thought of that name in many, many years. Now, it brought back a number of memories: hot, steamy nights in high school, parking next to the Vineyard Sound, and kissing until the morning. She'd had to sneak back into the very house she sat in now just before dawn to make sure her mom and dad hadn't caught her.

Yes. Scott Frampton was a name that did ring a bell.

Chapter Six

I t didn't take long for Aunt Kerry to announce that she'd cooked her famous New England clam chowder that morning and was ready to eat. Uncle Trevor rubbed his palms together. "I don't think I've ever been more famished."

"He says that almost every single day," Aunt Kerry said. "He doesn't know that it's up to him to head over, pick up the girls and the chowder, and bring everyone and the food back here."

Uncle Trevor grumbled. "It's always something with you, woman." His eyes sparkled with love for her, though, as he cut up and ruffled her perfect white bob.

Wes's eyes again turned toward the bay window and seemed to grow lost in the ocean view just beyond. Susan watched him contemplatively as Uncle Trevor discussed more of the specifics of dinner. "Yes, make sure you pick up the rolls from the bakery. Not the ones with seeds. Please, tell Charlotte and Claire not to bring any plates or bowls—there's enough of everything here. Oh, but we seem to need forks. Wes, what on earth have you done with all your cutlery over the years?"

Wes appeared not to have heard her. Aunt Kerry seemed accustomed to this behavior from him, although it chilled Susan to the bone as she continued to watch her. Uncle Trevor made a final note to himself on a tiny notepad and then bid them all goodbye. "I'll be back in two shakes of a lamb's tail."

When he disappeared, Susan tried to drum up some kind of conversation topic. Anything that would make her feel less like an outcast who hadn't returned to the home she left many, many eons ago. Aunt Kerry's grin faltered. If Susan knew anything, she knew that her aunt hadn't slept well over the past few days. Whatever act she had put on for Susan, it was about to fail.

But they didn't have long to wait. Soon, Trevor arrived with his two youngest daughters, Charlotte and Claire, who had set about making the side fixings for the late lunch. Again, Susan felt a punch to the stomach at the sight of them: two of her beautiful cousins with lives of their own and stories she hadn't yet heard. She hugged each of them for a long time and then fell into easy banter. Susan remembered that Charlotte had lost her husband in a fishing accident the year before, something she'd only learned on social media— but they didn't touch on this subject at all. Claire was still married to Russel Whalen, and they had twin girls, Abby and Gail, who Aunt Kerry and Uncle Trevor clearly adored. Their names came up several times throughout their dinner.

Together, Charlotte, Claire, Uncle Trevor, Aunt Kerry, Susan, and Wes sat at the table near the bay window. Aunt Kerry doted on each of them separately, making sure they each filled their bowls with an unreasonable amount of chowder. With each spoonful, Susan felt yanked back to other memories, long days when her mother and Aunt Kerry had slaved away in the kitchen for holiday events as she and the cousins and her sisters had rattled around this house or another, making endless chaos.

Now, she was a solid-as-a-rock adult.

"My god, Aunt Kerry, you must share this recipe with me. Your clam chowder was always the best." Susan said as she ate another spoonful.

"And how is it going in Newark, then, Susan?" Charlotte asked. She was chipper, her spoon poised over her half-eaten chowder.

"I actually don't know when I'll go back," Susan said, surprising herself with her own certainty. It had rolled around in her mind for several hours, but she hadn't expected the words to fly out like that.

"Oh? Can you do all your criminal law stuff from here?" Claire asked, raising an eyebrow.

Aunt Kerry blinked wide eyes at her. Susan swallowed and placed her napkin over her lips. Everyone's eyes were upon her, earnest and sure and kind. Still, she didn't feel ready to divulge the secrets of her previous years to them like this. In some respects, even though they were her family, they felt like people that were ghosts from her past.

"I'm terribly sorry. I just got so dizzy. I guess it must be from all the travel," she heard herself say. "Do you mind if I take a moment upstairs? I need to give Christine a call anyway."

Family always overcompensated. Charlotte and Claire spouted, "Of course! Take as much time as you need!" in almost perfect musical harmony. Aunt Kerry insisted that she take a glass of wine upstairs with her. "Don't be afraid to ask us for whatever you need. I know you've traveled a long way and must be overwhelmed by all this."

"I'm really fine. I just need to take a few minutes." Susan felt as though she spoke the words underwater. They bubbled around her and then got lost. She gripped the base of the wineglass stem, turned, and cut up the stairs. As she went, the smells of old lavender, of thirty-year-old carpet, of what might have been light mold, of cedar chests and old sweaters swirled around her. When she paused at the top of the landing, her heart grew so heavy she thought it might drop out of her stomach.

At the top of the landing, she blinked out to see the doorways to three bedrooms. At the far end of the hall was the bathroom. The large bedroom had been her parents'. If she clenched her eyes tight enough, she could almost hear their soft voices, muttering to each other in the middle of the night.

Christine and Lola had shared the bedroom nearest to the landing. The door was closed, and Susan couldn't bring herself to yank it open. The door on the opposite side of the hallway had been hers with a view of the forest. Guided by some strange, unseen force, Susan wrapped her hand around the golden knob and turned it.

When she entered her old bedroom, her knees clacked together beneath her. It looked exactly the same as it had fifteen years ago—when it had been exactly the same as it had been on the day Christine had left. Christine had taken over the room after Susan had headed off the island as the eldest sister. This meant the decor was a strange mix of Susan and Christine as disgruntled teenagers who'd just lost their mother. Music posters hung on the walls—Mazzy

Star, Alanis Morrissette, and Cat Power. A little board on the wall held various notes Christine had written to herself before she'd left. Things like: "Graduation party for Mark at 1," and, "Tennis practice at 4, don't be late!!!" The papers were faded and yellow, relics from a forgotten time.

The only addition to the room was the photographs on top of the old wardrobe. The photos were various ones Susan had sent to Wes during the early years of her motherhood before she had returned to Martha's Vineyard fifteen years before and decided never to speak to him again. This meant the photos acted as a time capsule. Amanda, age five, wearing overalls—and Jacob, age eight, in his baseball uniform. Susan lifted both and blew off the dust. It made her heart lurch, knowing that her dad had kept these photos all these years, even after she had stormed out angrily.

She'd only been away from Newark for less than twenty-four hours, and already, she missed her babies so much.

How had Wes felt knowing he might never see his babies again?

Susan dropped onto the edge of the bed she had once slept in and looked at her phone for a long time. She hadn't seen Christine in, what, five years? Six? Lola had passed through Newark two years ago, but all they'd done was have a brief dinner that had consisted of small talk and nothing else.

Neither Christine nor Lola posted much on social media, either. Susan had almost no idea what either of their lives looked like. Did they have romantic partnerships? Jobs? Were they happy? Did they ever think about her, about the Vineyard, about their father?

Was it too late to make up for everything?

She called Lola first. Lola was the hotheaded youngest sister who—last Susan had checked—worked as a journalist in Boston, frequently traveled, and ran through men like lightning. She was beautiful, bohemian, and whip-smart. Strangely, she felt like less of a wild card when Susan considered Christine.

Lola picked up on the fourth ring.

"Hello?" She sounded disgruntled, distrustful. She knew who was on the phone but didn't seem to want to give herself away.

"Hey, Lola. It's me. Susan."

There was a strange silence between them, which boosted the sound of live music in the background of wherever Lola was. Now that Lola's daughter was off to college, Susan suspected that Lola spent a lot of her off-work time "out."

"You'll never guess where I'm standing," she finally said. Her voice creaked.

"I guess not," Lola returned.

Susan clenched her phone tightly. "I'm in my childhood bedroom on the Vineyard. Dad is downstairs. Aunt Kerry made her famous chowder. Charlotte and Claire are here too."

Still, Lola didn't speak. There was a mutter, then a cough. It seemed as if she strained to get out of whatever crowd she sat in the middle of. Finally, the music faded, as did the flurry of conversation.

"Sorry. I was in the middle of a crowd," Lola said. Her voice remained hard-edged. "I thought you said you're back at Dad's house."

"I did," Susan said. Her heart surged with adrenaline.

She felt the stirrings of an approaching fight, although she hadn't a clue why.

"And you just wanted to call me? Because you feel nostalgic?" Lola asked in an overwhelming tone.

Susan rolled her eyes. "If you were here, you would be too."

"Well, I'm not. And that's kind of been on purpose," Lola retorted.

Susan swallowed. "I came because Aunt Kerry called me. Dad was in the hospital. He has dementia, and it's gotten pretty bad in the last few months. He can't live alone anymore."

Again, the silence was deafening. Susan sighed and let her shoulders fall. "Listen, I know this is a lot at once. Trust me. I just—I need you and Christine to come here when you can. The house, the inn, our family—it's all falling apart. I need your help to fix it. I want to fix us too. Please."

Lola made her wait another few seconds before she answered. Her voice was a bit softer but still resistant. "Okay. I'll look at my schedule tomorrow and let you know when I can. If I even can. I don't know."

"Okay, fair enough." This was really all Susan could have asked for.

Minutes later, Susan tried and failed to call Christine, who lived in New York City. Christine didn't answer. Susan had no clear picture of what Christine might have been up to. She pressed her phone to her chest, thinking as she blinked at the turquoise ocean beyond the forest outside her window. Beautiful smudges of coral, lavender, and a fiery orange blended together in the sky above to create an astounding sight that swept her away from all her worries at that moment. Finally, she realized all she could do was send her sister a text.

> Susan: Christine, hey. It's Susan. I'm at the Vineyard. Dad's sick—I'll explain when you call. The inn has fallen into disrepair, and I need your help. I'm asking you and Lola to come to Oak Bluffs as soon as you can. I know that might not be as soon as I would like. Just let me know when you can.

Chapter Seven

Susan woke in her childhood bed the next morning just after six thirty. She blinked at the ceiling, a crack that had grown longer and thicker in the years since she'd last slept there. The house creaked and drifted with the early-morning spring wind. Today was the first day of June. Somehow, someway, it was the first spring after Susan's divorce and her first full day on the island.

Downstairs on the breakfast table sat a basket of freshly baked croissants, biscuits, and blueberry muffins. A pot of coffee had recently been brewed, the smell of which stirred with the lilacs and baked bread. Wes Sheridan had always been an early riser. With Sunrise Cove, there had always been a reason to stay up late or wake up early.

"Dad?" Susan called out. There was no answer. Immediately, fear overwhelmed her. Wasn't this the common trope with dementia patients? They wandered off, got confused, and ended up somewhere lost and alone? She fled toward the door that looked out over the

50

road. Nothing. She rushed outside, her feet falling against the grass, wet with dew, then bounded around the side of the house. Again, she called for her father, her gaze scanning the trees. Had he wandered inside, looking for wood scraps for the bonfire?

But no. When she reached the water-side of the house, she found her father in a familiar spot. He was on the other porch swing, the one that remained attached to the porch itself. He swung with a cup of coffee in his hands as he gazed out at the water. He hadn't heard her frantic attempts to call.

Susan walked up the steps that led onto the porch. Once on the landing, her dad turned his head. His eyes brightened. "There she is. I thought you would never get up."

Susan chuckled. "You know it's only six forty-five, right?"

"Half the day is already over!" He smiled up at his daughter.

"Ha." Susan collected his coffee cup, returned to the house, refilled his, and grabbed herself some. Then, she brought out the basket of croissants, muffins, and biscuits and perched them on the little table in front of the porch swing. She sank her teeth into the buttery wonder of the fluffy croissant and closed her eyes, savoring the glorious taste. She hadn't eaten so gluttonously in years. There had been such pressure to look a certain way as a criminal lawyer in Newark—and Richard's wife. She had trimmed off any extra fluff over the years with endless pilates classes and early morning jogs.

"How does it feel to be back, then?" Wes tore the top off a biscuit and ate it slowly.

"It's difficult to describe," Susan answered. "Like no

time has passed. Or like three hundred years have passed."

"I've never understood time," Wes returned. "Sometimes, I sit out here, and I still think I can hear you girls running around in the woods, playing hide-and-go-seek."

Susan was breathless for a second. She felt she could hear the voices too. She considered telling her father there was a possibility her sisters would arrive sometime soon—but she didn't want to get his hopes up without more details.

"I hate that I've been away for so long," Susan said. "They always tell you when you're younger about the regrets you'll have when you're older. But you don't take the advice seriously until it's too late. I've missed this place. I know every single path on this island. I know the way the light hits the water. I know the air and the people and the food and..." She paused and pressed her lips together. "I know it in ways that I don't even know my own life back in Newark anymore."

Wes placed the uneaten half of his biscuit back in the basket. He seemed contemplative but unwilling to say what was on his mind. He swallowed a gulp of coffee.

"I just missed you, is all," Susan stated and patted his free hand.

But her dad didn't want to hear it anymore. He arched his brow in that same way he always had when he was tired of something and said, "I have to get over to the Cove soon. Want to come with me?"

"Of course I do," Susan said as she stole a glance at him. "How has it really been going over there?"

"It's better than ever," her dad said. "I hired a different lady to work at the front desk a few years back. Natalie. She's about thirty-five, I guess, and really whip-smart. Has a few kids of her own. Anyway, she told me yesterday that we're already booked solid for the entire summer—a real banner year for us."

"That's incredible, Dad. When we passed by yesterday, I couldn't help but..." She stopped, unsure if she should press forward.

Her dad flashed his eyes toward her. "What is it?"

"It just looked like it needed a little sprucing up, is all. I don't know if you hire the same people for spring cleaning?"

"I did it all myself the past few years. They changed management and started to rip me off. You know I don't have much patience for that," Wes said.

Admittedly, in Susan's memory, her father had little patience for anything. Her smile fluttered down, and she looked at the water for a bit. It was obvious that her dad didn't want to talk about any kind of neglect at the inn. The silence stretched between them. Was this really the life she wanted to return to? Full-time?

"I guess it's about that time," her father said. "Ready?"

Susan showered and dressed quickly and met her father back downstairs. He wore the same jean jacket he'd always worn, its gold buttons as bright and shiny as ever. He remained trim and physically healthy. He grabbed the house keys as Susan checked to ensure everything was off in the kitchen. She didn't want another fire incident.

Outside, Wes and Susan struck off down the once-familiar path that led from their house to the Sunrise Cove Inn. In the beginning, the path was lined with beautiful trees and caught a view of the water every few seconds, a reminder that it was never far from sight. Then, the edge of Oak Bluffs perked up, beautiful little streets with gorgeous houses that looked like gingerbread homes in different colors. Between the cafés and ice cream parlors, horse and buggies were carting tourists already, despite the earliness of the morning. Everything was already bustling.

As Susan continued to walk alongside her father, she couldn't help but remember all the high-end eateries to choose from, along with the ice cream parlors. The vineyard was always cool and casual, and being on the ocean was always an inspiration for the island chefs. The one thing about the Vineyard was the people on the island always ate well and never went without.

The Sunrise Cove Inn had a massive porch that wrapped nearly around the entirety of the building, with several porch swings that looked out over the water. The inn itself sat atop a slight hill. From there, sterling gray rocks reflected the sunlight piled toward the beach below. Between the rocks was a little pathway with a staircase that allowed easy water access. Susan stood on the inn's porch and gazed out at the beach while the winds rolled up the waves and cast them across the shore. Again, she could see them: herself, Christine, and Lola, holding hands and leaping into the water and shrieking at how cold it was.

Out in the blue, she recognized a little boat with a man she had once known. Stan, wasn't it? Stan Ellis. He had been a friend of her parents, a fisherman. He looked a bit more haggard, his back in a perfect curve as he yanked a line out from the water to bring up the perfect glitter of a fish. The motion was so timeless, like poetry. Susan held her breath as she stared.

Her father's feet creaked over the floorboards as he approached behind her.

"Isn't that Stan Ellis?" she asked without looking over at him.

"Guess it is," her dad returned. "I haven't talked to him in a while."

Susan followed her father through the front door. Just like the exterior, the interior seemed neglected as well. The same couches lined the waiting area, now forlorn-looking and slightly torn. The front desk was clean yet ragged. Standing with a phone to her ear was the new front desk concierge, Natalie: blond and smiley. She placed the phone back on its hook and said, "Goodness, you must be Susan. It's wonderful to finally meet you."

"And you!" Susan returned.

They shook hands. Natalie looked as though she might bubble over.

"Wes has talked so much about his girls I feel like I know you already," Natalie said.

Susan felt a bit struck by the comment. She forced a wider smile. Wes pressed his hand across the top of the front desk and said, "I have a little meeting with some staff. Do you mind if I step away for a moment?"

Susan realized he spoke to her. Flustered, she said, "Oh, I don't mind. No. Go ahead."

This left Susan with Natalie. Natalie continued to beam at her. This was a stark difference from anyone Susan normally dealt with in Newark. It was optimistic and pure.

"The inn seems like it needs a little bit of... help," Susan said suddenly as her eyes continued to scan the front lobby.

Natalie's eyes flashed around confusedly. "Oh? Do you think so?"

Susan's stomach clenched. "It just doesn't seem the

same as it did when I was younger. Maybe it works for the people who come? Dad said that you're already booked up for the summer."

"Yes, we are! We used internet advertising and got people in from all over the place." She grinned. "I took a marketing class online and learned a thing or two. Your dad hardly knows how to use a computer, if you can believe it!"

"Oh, I believe it." Susan's smile became a bit more natural. Maybe she could use Natalie to better understand the common occurrences at the inn and why it seemed so rough around the edges. "You know about my dad's diagnosis, don't you?"

Natalie's face turned gray. "Yes. He only told me a few months ago. Of course, I noticed things around the inn—things that I had to pick up the slack for. But I was more than willing to do it. And still am. The thing is, I don't know much about business beyond what that marketing class taught me. And Wes has been in the hospitality business for as long as he's been alive."

"I'm going to pick up some of that slack," Susan told her.

"Oh! So you're staying, then?"

"I think so. For the time being, until I figure everything out."

"Then I look forward to being your friend, Susan." Natalie nodded at her. Again, her words were welcoming and sweet.

Susan headed to her father's office after that to wait for him. Her father's office was also a relic—something of an expected thing, she supposed—with furniture from the '80s, a family portrait from maybe 1992 hanging on the wall (with styles that suited those times), and a massive desktop computer from probably 2002 atop the old desk. To his credit, the office remained clean and orderly. Engraved into the side of the desk remained the words— as always—Wes and Anna Sheridan. This had been the desk they had worked at together for as long as Susan could remember. This had been their office.

The office had a little porch overlooking the ocean and a fishing pier. Susan stood out and closed her eyes, feeling the fresh blast of the salty ocean wind whip across her cheeks and blow around her long chocolate locks around her face. When she opened her eyes again, she spotted Stan a bit further out. It seemed crazy to her that all the people on this island were doing the same things, performing the same tasks, even working on the same computer, for decades.

"There she is!' Her father's voice boomed out from the doorway. A bit of color had returned to his cheeks. He looked vibrant and happy, the way he always had when he'd taken charge of something.

"Just catching as much as I can of this beautiful view," Susan said. "I can't believe I haven't seen it in so many years."

Again, her father seemed unwilling to dip into any kind of nostalgia. He nodded, maintaining his smile, and said, "I have a few more meetings during the morning. Do you want to meet back at the bistro at noon for lunch? The chef we've had for the past eight or nine months is to die for. I think you might have known him in high school."

This piqued Susan's curiosity. How many other people had stayed on the island from her past? She agreed to meet her dad in an hour and decided to wander through town to check out the old sights until then.

Chapter Eight

Once outside the inn, Susan wandered toward the downtown area of Oak Bluffs—down Lake Avenue toward the police station and the Oak Bluffs Ferry Dock. It was still early, around nine, but Oak Bluffs didn't know any better and had erupted into a gorgeous, busy day. Susan couldn't help but feel the infectious energy of the vibrant tourists, the wide smiles, and the laughter. She paused at a little coffee stand to buy another cup and then sat to people-watch for a while with the sunlight beaming down upon her. While there, she remembered to text Amanda about her internship. Amanda responded that she was going to be "busier than ever" but was so excited to dig into a few actual cases that summer.

> Amanda: How is the Vineyard?

> Susan: Eerily the same.

Susan sent a picture of her current view of the water and the ferries.

> Susan: Wish you were here. Maybe later in the summer?

> Amanda: How long are you staying? How is Grandpa?

It was all too difficult to explain just then, though. Susan's thumbs hovered over the phone as she pondered how to phrase this.

"Susan! Hey! I didn't think I'd find you out here today."

Susan flipped her head up to find her cousin Claire standing before her with several enormous bouquets of flowers in her outstretched arms. Claire owned a flower shop, which she had briefly discussed at lunch the day before.

"Wow! So funny to run into you. What are you up to?"

"My delivery guy called in sick," Claire said. "I'm a bit exhausted. Was up all night making the last of these bouquets, and now I have to deliver them! Luckily, I'm taking the rest of the day off."

"Let me come with you," Susan offered.

"What? You don't have to do that," Claire returned.

"I have some time to kill. Dad has some meetings this morning. Besides, it's a good way to see more of Oak Bluffs. My eyes are so hungry for all the beautiful things here. You might not know this, but Newark isn't exactly known for its beauty."

Claire laughed and passed several bouquets to Susan, who adjusted them easily in her outstretched arms. Lilacs, lilies, daffodils, baby's breath: the smells swirled and filled her nostrils.

"I can't believe this is your job. It's like a dream," Susan admitted as they walked together.

"Ha. It's funny you should say that. My sisters, brother, and I always talk about how jealous we are of your life! You, Christine, and Lola got out of here and experienced the rest of the world. All I know is this island and these flowers. That's it."

"Trust me. It's better here," Susan admitted.

Claire chuckled. "You've been away for a long time. I bet you've forgotten a lot of the bad. Although..." She paused, reflecting. "You and your dad seem to be doing better?"

Of course. It was common knowledge that the Sheridan sisters didn't adore their father.

"Like you said, it's been a long time. I want to let it all go," Susan said.

There was a funny quiver in her stomach—a hesitation.

Could she get away with skating through these feelings without analyzing them and picking them apart?

Still, it didn't seem like her dad wanted to have any real discussion. He wouldn't even admit that the inn looked a little raggedy.

"You said your sisters are coming in, right?" Claire asked. "Lola and I used to have the wildest times. I've missed her a lot."

"Right. You guys were closest in age. I remember that, now," Susan said. She cleared her throat. How was it that the flowers had begun to feel heavy?

"I haven't spoken with Lola in about six months? Something like that?" Claire continued.

Susan felt another lurch. Claire obviously kept in better contact with Lola than Susan did. "They don't know when they'll be able to make it. But they need to be here. Dad's obviously not doing well. The inn is a mess. It's just time."

Claire nodded. "I would have called you sooner if Mom hadn't told me not to."

Susan furrowed her brow. "Really?"

"It's just that we thought all of you were done with this place. And after all that you three went through, it's not like we blamed you," Claire said.

Susan and Claire delivered the bouquets throughout the next half hour. The conversation fluttered off to other things. Claire told Susan about Charlotte's difficulty with her husband's death. "I wasn't sure she would ever get out of that depression, but she seems to be doing a tiny bit better now," Claire said. Susan mentioned her divorce, but only briefly. Claire said she figured that had been the case since Susan hadn't brought Richard up at all throughout the meal the day before.

"But if he didn't know how to keep Susan Sheridan in his life, then what kind of man is he?" Claire asked. "Everyone always knew that you were the biggest catch this island had."

"That's totally not true," Susan said, looking at her with a smirk.

"Come on. It is. You dated, like, every guy in high school. You drove Scott nuts until he had you all to himself for those last few years. But he always knew that he couldn't keep you. Not forever. You were meant for bigger things," Claire said with assurance.

Susan and Claire returned to the flower shop together. As they walked, they passed by several people she had once known—all of whom greeted Claire and then burst with, "My goodness, aren't you Susan Sheridan?" She was surprised to note how pleased she was to be recognized.

"It feels like a welcoming parade," she joked to Claire.

"Now you know the gossip will really start to swirl," Claire said with a smile.

When they entered the flower shop, Claire's twin girls, Abby and Gail, were perched at the front desk. At fourteen, both were tall and wiry, with gorgeous brown hair that reflected the sunlight streaming in from the ocean-view window. Abby was in the middle of braiding Gail's hair while Gail chewed absently at a piece of gum and flipped through a magazine.

The entire scene reminded Susan so much of herself and her sisters that she nearly collapsed.

"Girls, I want you to meet someone," Claire announced, getting their attention. "This is my dear cousin, Susan. She grew up on the island but hasn't been back since you girls were born."

Abby and Gail gave a sing-song, "Hello!" before returning their eyes to the magazine and hair combo.

"They man the front desk for me when I run errands," Claire explained. "Sometimes, they do deliveries for me, but it's good for me to get my steps in."

"She's always talking about her step count," Abby said, giggling.

Claire tousled Abby's hair. "You're getting good at that French braid. You'll have to do me next."

"You know, I saw Stan Ellis out fishing today on the water," Susan said suddenly. "Do you remember that guy? I guess he must be around my dad's age."

Claire's eyes grew hazy. "Yes, of course. The old fisherman. He generally keeps to himself."

"It was so weird to remember him today. I haven't thought about him in twenty-five years," Susan said.

"I guess that'll be a constant over the next few weeks," Claire said.

After that, Susan walked back to the inn to meet her father for lunch. As she walked, her phone buzzed twice —once from Christine, the next from Lola. She assumed the two of them had been on the phone, probably going over the details of a potential Martha's Vineyard trek.

Christine: Sorry I missed your call, sis. I can't believe you're there. I have some loose ends to tie up in NYC, but I'll get there as soon as I can. Probably in a few days.

Lola: I have to finish covering a story before I can skip out of Boston. I'll keep you posted.

Susan couldn't blame her sisters for their hesitation. She would have been just as hesitant if her entire life hadn't just exploded before Aunt Kerry had called her there.

When Susan reached the bistro, Wes sat at his long-time favorite table toward the back wall with a full view of the water. He had his hands cupped under his chin and seemed again lost in thought. What were the thoughts of a person with dementia? The idea troubled her, but she shoved it away.

When she sat, he perked up and dropped his hand over hers.

"Hey, Dad. How were the meetings?"

"Not too bad. I have to take really diligent notes these days." He tapped his temple with a finger. "The second I know something, I don't know it anymore. The Dr. said it's only going to get worse. I feel all slippery."

He grinned, clearly hoping this could be some kind of joke for her. Susan matched his smile, although she didn't feel it. She told him a bit about seeing Claire and her two girls. "They're so big! I can't believe I've never met them."

Susan and her dad both ordered water and a starter salad from one of the bistro servers, a teenage girl who'd clearly grown up on the island.

"So, you said you might stick around for a while?" her dad said once the server had taken their orders and disappeared.

"That's the plan," Susan returned. "I guess I didn't mention this, but Richard and I were just divorced. Six months ago."

Her father's stoic face remained unchanged. He spread his hands across the white tablecloth and took a slow breath. "I see."

Was that judgment in his voice? Anger? Susan's first instinct was to think her father was on the verge of some sort of angry tirade, like in the old days.

But instead, his words were soft and tranquil.

"It's a sad thing, divorce. I'm sorry you have to go through this. When raising kids, you hope they never have to endure any pain. And then you realize that one of the only things life gives out for sure is pain," he said.

Susan nodded and bit down on her lower lip. "It's for the best. It really is. It's just going to take some getting used to. Even looking at my bare ring finger is strange. And—I'm forty-four years old. It's both young and not young. It's somewhere in the middle."

"You're in a transition. As am I," her father stated like the wise old man he was.

"I guess you're right."

"And perhaps we can wage war on our transitions together," he said, smiling at her.

"I like the sounds of that," Susan returned.

Her heart felt light. Their salads arrived as her father explained some of the numbers about the inn and bistro—all of which seemed to indicate that all was right as rain. Perhaps this easy life of sunshine and family was the only therapy she really needed. Perhaps everything would be all right, after all.

Chapter Nine

Scott Frampton marched off the freight behind his older brother, Chuck, and cast his gaze toward the bliss of a bustling island afternoon. Chuck grunted as he shot up into the waiting truck, filled with the last of their supply for the morning and early afternoon. He smeared his arm across his forehead to wipe away the beads of sweat that had formed from the morning sun. The last few restaurants, hotels, and other tourist havens awaited their weekly supplies—and Scott knew they were anxious. After all, he and Chuck were about an hour late due to especially violent waves. They'd had to keep things slow.

Chuck drove the truck away from the docked freight and clicked around on the radio. Chuck was a country music fan, and his whistle found the tune in seconds. Scott leaned his head back and closed his eyes for a second. It had been a tough night. His son, who lived in Boston with his mother, had struggled with his math homework and called Scott several times for help. Scott had never been what you might call a "stellar mathematician," so he had scoured the internet for pre-algebra help until after midnight. That wasn't the kind of thing a guy with a four thirty wake-up time should be doing, but they were, after all, dad duties that he couldn't just ignore.

Still, Scott liked the idea that he remained at least partially in his son's life. When his wife had taken him away, Scott had more or less resigned himself to the fact that his version of fatherhood wouldn't look the way he wanted it to.

"You heard that Wes Sheridan went to the hospital?" Chuck asked. He turned down the volume on the radio.

"No. It's gotten worse, then?" Scott and Chuck had noted Wes Sheridan's lackluster mental state as of late. They'd heard the rumors of dementia. This pretty much confirmed it.

"Guess so," Chuck returned.

"I wonder if his daughters know," Scott said.

Chuck clucked his tongue. In the wake of Wes's ailments, Scott had asked the older man if there was anything he could do to help out. He had noticed that the inn had grown increasingly dilapidated. In fact, he had spoken with several guests at the Sunrise Cove Inn who weren't pleased with their stay due to its current state. "It looked really different online," was how one guy had phrased it. This sort of talk cut Scott to the core. He had countless good memories in that inn.

He had even lost his virginity in one of the rooms.

Still, Chuck always said that Scott shouldn't care so much about other people's business. Scott tended toward nostalgia and empathy, but Chuck was the actionable of the two: a sturdy man who lacked passion but wasn't afraid of hard work. The two men balanced each other out; together, they had made their father's business much more profitable than ever before.

When they pulled up in front of the Sunrise Cove Inn, Scott hopped out and yanked open the back of the truck. Inside were stacks and stacks of wine bottles and beer kegs and frozen foods with flour, sugar, and yeast—all the things the attached bistro needed during the high tourist months. Chuck headed off to greet Zach, the main chef, while Scott began to carry things in. Zach Walters had gone to high school with Scott, although he had been younger. This meant he was maybe just over forty. He had only worked as a chef at the Sunrise Cove Inn for the previous nine months or so, since late-season when Wes had had to let the head chef go. The rumor was that Wes had gotten into many tiffs with the previous chef as a result of his diminishing health. Wes hadn't wanted to admit that he'd been ill. Once he had fired him, it had been too late.

Chuck and Scott piled up the boxes and kegs in the storage room. Zach yanked his white chef hat off and wiped his palm across his forehead. He gave Scott an exhausted grin.

"A big day?" Scott asked.

"I forgot how much it picks up during the season," Zach said. "And with Wes being in the hospital, it's been a rough few days."

"He's doing okay, though, yeah?" Scott asked.

"Sure. They discharged him yesterday. He's in the sitting area now if you want to go take a peek and say hi," Zach said. He gave Scott a peculiar smile.

"I have to run off and write up a few receipts for you guys," Chuck said as he looked at them. "I'll meet you back here in a bit." He gave Scott a gruff pat on the shoulder and disappeared into the main hotel lobby, where he normally helped Natalie write up the ledger and gave her receipts for what had been delivered since she was still pretty new.

"Go on. Say hi to Wes. I'm sure he would be happy to see you," Zach encouraged him again.

Scott arched his brow and headed out of the steamy kitchen. Once outside, he stood behind the pastry counter with a full view of the gorgeous bistro, with its baby-blue painted walls and its enormous window with a full view of the Nantucket Sound. Martha's Vineyard sat to the west of it. Scott's gaze fell toward the far window, where old Wes Sheridan sat in his familiar spot. He shared the table with a dark-haired woman who faced away from Scott.

Immediately when he spotted her, Scott's heart gave a peculiar thud, and he could feel a lump form in his throat.

The woman tilted her head. Wes said something, his face bright. The second he finished, the woman across from him erupted with laughter.

The laughter was a sound Scott hadn't heard since he was eighteen. He literally couldn't breathe and felt his knees lock beneath him. He felt transported through time and back to his high school days.

Susan. Susan Sheridan.

The love of his teenage years.

The girl who had gotten away.

He turned quickly and returned to the kitchen. Once inside, he leaned against the wall and watched as Zach Walters burst into laughter. His hat shook so hard it fell off again.

"You should see your face. You look like you just saw a ghost." He laughed.

"You set me up!" Scott shot.

Zach shrugged, tapping the sides of his eyes to get rid of his tears. "I have to make my own fun around here. You can't blame me."

"You knew she was here, and you just sent me out there to..."

"She looks good, Scott. Really good," Zach interrupted him.

"Who looks good?" Chuck entered again, his voice booming.

"Susan Sheridan is here," Zach affirmed.

Chuck drew a smug smile. "Oh, great. The prodigal girlfriend."

Rage swam through Scott. Still, he couldn't blame Chuck. It was true that when Susan had left him, left the island, Scott had gone on a kind of eighteen-year-old bender: hardly going a day without drinking too much, spending as many hours as he could out on the boat. He had fallen out of his life and away from everyone who had ever known him. She had taken a piece of him when she'd left.

Scott had always thought he would marry Susan.

And then, one day, she was just gone.

"Come on, man. Let's get out of here," Chuck said.

Scott felt strange leaving like that. Wasn't it more honest to stay and say hello? But still, what could he possibly say after so much time had passed between them? *I can't believe you had someone else's baby so soon after you left. I can't believe you betrayed everything we'd ever said to each other. I can't believe—*

But then again, Scott could believe it. The Sheridan

sisters had gone through hell and back. He had watched Susan fall into depression, unable to eat some days, always trying her best to keep her younger sisters afloat. She had gotten into countless fights with her father during those last months. Staying on the Vineyard hadn't been an option.

"She's trouble," Chuck said all of a sudden when they were back in the truck. "You know it too. It's why you didn't just casually go up to her and say hello. You know what she could do to you. She was such bad news back in the day. Always crying. Don't you remember? You had to miss a football game once because she..."

"Had a panic attack? Yeah, and I don't regret it either," Scott affirmed, his nostrils flaring. "She lost her mom. Things were really hard for her and her sisters. I was there for her as much as I could be."

"And then she chewed you up and spat you out," Chuck scoffed as he started to walk away.

"We were kids," Scott retorted.

Chuck lived a bit away from the water, deep in a forested area, while Scott had a little house close to the water on the outskirts of Oak Bluffs. They had lived together for a brief time after Scott's divorce; this had ended in a thrown beer bottle and a screaming match in the middle of the road. They'd rectified their differences since, however. They'd had to for the good of the freight business.

Chuck dropped Scott off and gave him a flat-palmed wave. Scott nodded back, then turned and walked up into his house. The water crashed on the sand and rocks, filling Scott's ears. He entered the kitchen area, grabbed a beer from the refrigerator, and then returned to the porch swing. Out there, he spotted old Stan Ellis in his fishing boat. The man spent most of the summer out there, far from people, far from conversation. Most people knew what he had done. Most people didn't want anything to do with him.

Most people were okay with pretending that he didn't exist.

Still, there he was, and there Scott sat—both alone. For the first time, Scott saw himself the way others might have seen him—just a disgruntled, lonely old man who operated a freighting business and then returned home for a single afternoon beer. What sort of life had he lived so far? And what would Susan think if she knew him this way?

Chapter Ten

After lunch, Susan's father announced he felt pretty tired and needed to lie down. Susan helped him to his feet and was surprised when he staggered a bit. As they walked past the glass case filled with pastries, the kitchen door flashed open to reveal a familiar face.

"Zach Walters. Is that you?" Susan asked with a smile.

"As I live and breathe," Zach returned. He was just as handsome as ever, with bright blue eyes, a mischievous grin, and dark, tousled blond hair. He also had the cutest dimple on his right cheek when he smiled.

"You're the chef here? Dad said it was someone from high school, but I couldn't have imagined it being you."

"Yep. Since late last summer," Zach said. "I went to culinary school in Boston and worked there for a few years before returning. I can't complain at all. It's a fantastic place to work."

"I should hope so!" Susan said as she nodded at him. Her mind buzzed through a few memories of Zach. He had been a few years younger, on the outskirts. If she remembered correctly, her sister Christine had hated him more than the devil himself, although she couldn't remember why.

They said goodbye to Zach and Natalie and walked the rest of the way back to the house. They chatted amicably, and her father told her a few other Vineyard gossip stories. He was so entrenched in the history of the place, a master of who had come and gone, died or married, given birth, created any art, or met anyone famous. He told her that Obama had eaten lunch one afternoon last year at the bistro with his family. Susan loved to fall into the familiar syllables of his words. She held his hand as they entered the house and squeezed it hard.

"Thank you for sharing lunch with me," she said. "Zach really knows his way around the kitchen."

"It was perfect, Susie. Thank you," he said just before he creaked up the steps to his bedroom.

Alone, Susan snagged a sparkling water from the fridge and returned to the porch to look out at the water. Running a hand through her hair, she felt strangely apprehensive. She told herself it was because she was so accustomed to the rush-rush, go-go of her normal criminal lawyer life in Newark. The Vineyard told her to slow down, to breathe in the salty air, but she resisted it.

She would have to relearn how to be a Vineyard woman.

The pain was something that came in waves. Just sometimes. A reminder. Susan heaved a sigh and grabbed her purse to find the contraption that would relieve some pain at that moment. She didn't want to be on any heavy pain meds, so her Dr. had given her a medical marijuana prescription. She hadn't had any of the stuff since her teenage years, and then only in small amounts with Scott. She inhaled with her eyes closed and felt the pain slowly drift away. Her shoulders dropped a bit as she eased into the calm of herself.

It would all be okay.

Hours had drifted by. She chatted with Amanda briefly on the phone while Amanda was on break from her internship. Jake had sent a hilarious photo of the twins. She texted back that her cousin, Claire, also had twins—a genetic thing, must be.

> Susan: I'm glad I didn't have to go through that. Double the diapers, double the fun!

> Jake: Don't remind me :)

Wes creaked down the steps just after five. He looked bleary-eyed but happy. Almost on cue, Aunt Kerry also appeared at the front door with a large pizza for the three of them to share from Offshore Ale Co. She yanked the cardboard top open to reveal a cheesy mess of sausage, mozzarella, peppers, and onions, all Susan and her dad's favorite toppings. Susan slid a greasy slab onto her plate and sat out on the picnic table on the porch with the two of them, genuinely shocked that she allowed herself to eat such a monstrous portion.

It was okay, though. This was her life now. She would do whatever she wanted as long as she was there, where she was needed.

After she had eaten, there was a creak of tires over the stones that covered the driveway out front. Wes's ears perked up.

"Who could that be?"

"No idea," Aunt Kerry said. She stood and marched inside, headed toward the door that opened out toward the driveway. But before she could reach it, the door burst open.

This was the way of the Vineyard. Once you belonged anywhere, you belonged there for life—and just entered through the door when you wanted. Susan had forgotten that.

"SUSIE? Is Susan Sheridan here?"

Susan shot up and peered through the window to see two very familiar faces. They came into focus all too soon as Lily Walton and Sarah Brown rushed out onto the porch. They had been her very best friends from the earliest days of her life, all the way to her eighteenth year. Tears sprung to her eyes as they wrapped themselves around her and jumped up and down like high school girls.

"We heard you were here!" Lily cried. She fell back and grinned broadly. Her prominent freckles danced across the bridge of her nose, and her red curls bounced. "I told Sarah that it couldn't be possible. That you said, you'd never be back here. But here you are!"

"We had to come to see for ourselves," Sarah said. She was curvy and blond, with vibrant blue eyes that seemed to swallow everything. "And here you are!"

Susan was overwhelmed with emotion. In some ways, having these two girls in her arms again made her feel safer than she had in years. In others, she felt dizzy with guilt. She hadn't called. She had hardly messaged. She hadn't been there for marriages or babies or even a funeral. She had been a ghost. And here they were, welcoming her back.

"Lily and Sarah!" Wes said with a wide grin. "It's so

76

good to see you girls back at my house. Although I have to say, things have been much quieter around here without any hijinks from you three."

"Like that time we set off those fireworks," Lily said mischievously.

"We just wanted to see what would happen," Sarah said.

"You nearly set fire to the dog!" Wes cried as he beamed at them.

Everyone burst into laughter. Of course, the dog had not ever been in any kind of real danger, but the dog, whose name was Missy, had whined and cried the rest of the night as a kind of punishment.

"Poor baby," Susan said.

"You have to come out with us," Lily said then. "Seriously. We've decided that we won't take no for an answer. I've had to babysit Heather's baby all day, and I want to cut loose!"

"Heather had a baby?" Susan gasped, looking from friend to friend. "I didn't know."

"Heather is very strict about social media," Lily explained. "Told me I couldn't post anything about baby Remy. Oh, but I love her to pieces!" She flashed up her phone to show the gorgeous, fat-cheeked baby.

Aunt Kerry agreed to hang at the house with Wes, which cleared Susan to rush back to Lily's pickup truck and whisk her out into the warm spring night. As they raced down the road, she felt free and alive, much more like a sixteen-year-old girl with her best friends than a forty-four-year-old woman fresh off a divorce.

Lily yanked the truck off to the edge of Oak Bluffs, toward a little cove they had frequently swum in as teens. Susan was surprised to see that the cove was empty.

"Haven't other teenagers taken our spot by now?" she asked as she hopped out of the truck.

"I put a spell around it," Sarah said, chuckling. "Nobody else can find it unless they know where it is."

"A secret spell." Susan laughed.

"Speaking of spells..." Lily said as she reached into the back of the truck and pulled out two bottles of rosé and three wineglasses. "I figured we could have a little spell while we're here in our sacred place."

It was too good to be true. Night came fast, spinning a gorgeous haze of pinks, yellows, purples, and blues over the top of the crystalline water. Sarah spread out a picnic blanket, and the three women sat and poured glasses. There was chaos in the air as they lifted their glasses and clinked.

"To us being back together again," Susan whispered. "Thank you for coming to find me. It means the world."

They sipped their wine and hung in the silence for a moment. Where should they begin? How could Susan possibly update them on so, so many years of her life?

"I can't believe you're here," Lily said quietly. She strung a strand of red hair behind her ear.

"Neither can I. If you had told me a week ago that I would be here today, I wouldn't have believed you. But Dad, he's..."

"Yeah. We heard," Sarah said.

"I guess I'm the last to know," Susan said with a sigh. "Not that I blame anyone for keeping it from me. I wanted to run away as fast as I could. And now... I regret that."

"You shouldn't," Lily insisted. "Everyone understands that you had to go off and find something else. Everyone gets it. Really."

Susan pushed the girls to tell her more about their lives. Lily talked about how incredulous she was about being a grandmother. "Vincent is off at college, of course. Yale. He was always such a smart kid. I know he didn't get that from me. Definitely from my father."

Lily's father had been a longtime whale-watching expert. Before his death, he'd been the historical expert on island and water life. Susan had read that he had died. Had she written Lily about it? She couldn't remember now.

"Oh, Lily. Your dad. It's so strange coming back to the island without him here. I'm so sorry for your loss," Susan said, her brow furrowed.

"He was so sick at the end that it was really a blessing," Lily explained. Her eyes grew dense with tears. "I miss him every single day, of course. He never got to be a great-grandfather, bless him!"

The girls continued to drink and exchange stories.

"I met Peter in New York," Sarah said. "I think you knew I was there for a while, right? Anyway, I went to school at NYU and majored in art. As my parents said at the time—a huge waste of time and money! Probably, they were right. Anyway, I dragged Peter back to the Vineyard with me after I grew tired of the city, and we never looked back."

"She has her own art studio here on the island now," Lily said.

Susan was incredulous. "I remember you took a few art classes in high school, but I didn't know it would turn into this. That is remarkable, Sarah. I'm so happy for you."

"Maybe you remember meeting my two babies?" Sarah continued, looking hopeful.

Susan had a bleary memory of that fateful trip fifteen years ago when she had seen Sarah in the middle of her toddler-baby-chaos. "Dax. And Ellen. They must be..."

"Sixteen and seventeen, respectively," Sarah said, beaming. "A different sort of life. I think it's going to be really hard to say goodbye."

Susan laughed and felt her eyes well with tears. "You don't even know."

Susan described the details of her divorce to her two oldest and dearest best friends. The women said all the right things at all the right times and seemed overly willing to head to Newark to burn his house down. Susan told them, through gasped laughter, that this wasn't necessary.

"You know what we should do?" Lily asked conspiratorially.

"Not burn Richard's house down?" Susan said.

"No. I mean, maybe later. But right now—we should go swimming, just like we used to! It's always the best time to swim when the sky is all pink. The most romantic..." Lily continued.

A dock snaked out from the side of their cove area onto the gorgeous water. Together, the three women stripped down to their bra and underwear and walked, a bit bleary-eyed from wine, to the edge of the dock. They gripped hands and gazed out at the water. Susan felt her heart surge into her throat.

"Oh! Wait a minute. I forgot!" Lily said suddenly.

"What? What are you talking about?" Susan asked.

Lily tipped her head toward the shore. Above the dock, through a circle of trees, was a little one-story house with a veranda. A figure stood on the porch, gazing out at them with a beer in hand.

"Who is that man?" Susan asked. He was far enough away that she didn't mind standing only in her bra and underwear. Wasn't it just like a swimsuit, anyway?

Lily's grin widened. "Should I tell her, Sarah?"

"You're obviously going to, anyway."

Susan squeezed their hands harder. "Come on! What is going on?"

"That, darling Susan Sheridan, is Scott Frampton," Lily said, her voice whisper-like, conspiratorial. "What do you think about that?"

Susan's heart pumped with new life, and she stole one more glance. She squeezed their hands harder and harder, suddenly unable to think. But before fully verbalizing what she wanted to say, Lily leaped forward, yanking both other girls along with her. In a split second, they crashed into the water. There was frantic darkness. There was life. Kicking limbs and big thrusts to the surface, then a howl that it was "way colder than it should be!"

The girls rushed back to shore in under a minute. All the while, Susan felt the watchful eyes of the man she had once loved, far up on the porch between the trees.

They hadn't spoken or seen each other since they were eighteen. He didn't have social media. She knew nothing about him. Only that the thought of him still made her ache with the thought of what could have been.

Chapter Eleven

It wasn't like Susan to go along with a dare. For goodness' sake, she was a criminal lawyer, the sort of woman who did her own thing and danced to the beat of her own drum. But out on the shore that night, with the last pink haze shimmering over the ocean, she felt overcome with a sense of what could be. "Go talk to him. Now. We dare you." They were Lily's words, but they might as well have come from the universe itself.

Susan had had two glasses of wine. Her dark hair was drenched; her bra and underwear were soaked. She stretched her arms out on either side of her athletic frame. What would Scott think, seeing her like this? She could immediately recall the last day she'd seen him. She had told him about school and that she had decided to head off to college after all—despite having told him all summer long that she would remain to care for Lola and Christine. He had looked beaten. He hadn't begged her to stay. Scott had never been the type to do that. But he had told her he would love her for the rest of his life. She'd thought at the time that that was ridiculous.

Now, she understood what it meant to go through time. It didn't matter at all.

"What could I even wear?" she asked incredulously. Was she actually going to go through with this? Again, she felt the adrenaline of a much younger woman than her forty-four years.

Lily dragged her back to the truck, where Susan stripped herself of her bra and underwear and again donned the dress she'd had on earlier. Sans bra, she felt all loose and strange. But what the heck did she care? Scott had been the first person to see her like that, hadn't he? Plus, she was only going to say hello as quickly as she could—nothing more. She might not even get close enough for him to tell.

Sarah smacked her butt as she walked from the pickup toward Scott's. She reared around and gave her a big-eyed look.

"Why can't you ever behave yourself, Sarah?" she said teasingly.

"Go get 'em, champ," Sarah returned.

Susan tried to imagine telling this story to her daughter, Amanda. She imagined saying, "I jumped into the Nantucket Sound at dusk and then went over to talk to an old fling, without my makeup or hair done." Amanda would just look at her dumbstruck.

When she reached the base of the dock, she caught sight of Scott again. He stood in the same place on the porch, gazing out at the Sound with the beer in his hand. She took a deep breath and then approached the snaking staircase from the beach to the old weathered porch. She forced her eyes to find his as she approached.

And when his eyes returned her gaze, she stopped short. She couldn't take it. The impact was too much.

There he was. Not ten feet away from her. His blue eyes shone brightly, reflecting the Nantucket Sound itself, and his lips were turned upward, almost hopeful. He wore a black V-neck T-shirt, highlighting his broad shoulders and the roundness of his muscles. As a freight worker, he probably lifted heavy crates all day, every day, and it certainly showed.

She was totally breathless. Susan finally dropped her hands to her sides, suddenly remembering she had left her bra in the truck. Hurriedly, she drew her arms over her chest and crossed them.

"Susan Sheridan," he said. His voice was scratchy, deep—the same voice he'd had at eighteen, aged up for a man.

A shiver wound down her back. "Scott Frampton," she replied with a smile.

She had the funniest urge to run up the steps and collapse in his arms, the way she had so, so many years before. The way she had when her mother had died. He had been a constant figure in her life until she'd scrubbed him out.

Now, there they stood before each another—after all the bizarre years without each other. Currently just distant memories. All that mattered was the here and the now.

"I heard you were in town," Scott said. He took a step down from the porch, then another. He was barefoot, as any man might be who stood out on his porch, unsuspecting that his long-lost love might arrive.

"I heard you, um. We're here?" Susan chuckled loud enough for both of them to hear. "I'm sorry. I was over with Lily and Sarah, and we had a bit of wine, to be honest."

"It's okay. I've also imbibed," he said. He lifted his beer and cheered her. "I saw you jump off the dock. I hoped you would come and say hi."

Susan nodded. "Well, here I am."

Again, they studied each other. Susan decided that he actually looked excellent for forty-four years, much more handsome than he had been at eighteen.

"How have you been?" Susan finally sputtered. It felt both awkward and not, as though they wanted to play up the awkwardness for some kind of joke.

"I've been good. Just standing here in this spot for the past twenty-five years," Scott said. He smiled at her again, revealing the laugh lines around his eyes.

"You look good for so little exercise," Susan said, pointing at him.

"I do calf raises," he said.

"I hope you have someone to deliver your groceries?"

"Sure. But I eat an exclusive diet of mixed nuts," he half joked with her.

Susan belly-laughed, then. She had forgotten what it was like to stand before a man who actually made her laugh. Richard hadn't made her laugh—maybe ever? She couldn't remember anymore. Had she really gone twenty-five years without being with a man who made her laugh?

Not that it mattered now. Not that she even knew what Scott's situation was.

"The inn is falling apart," Susan said suddenly. She dropped her hands again, not sure she cared what Scott saw or didn't see. "And I don't know how to fix it. I'm sure you know about my dad, also. The dementia symptoms creep in and out. I never know how long I can leave him anywhere. I've only just arrived after fifteen years away, and already I feel like I'm in under my head."

"I've noticed the inn has been... how should I put this... neglected," Scott said. He scratched the back of his head and added, "But your father is a proud guy. He generally knows what he's doing. It's a disease that very few people really understand."

"But it also feels like with all the money that goes into that place, he should be able to afford to fix it up," Susan continued. "I don't know. I have to look at his accounting. He's probably let some numbers slip away. I'm not sure."

She hadn't planned to show this much emotion. She had wanted to say hello and then run back to her friends. That was it. But here she was, baring her soul to this guy —this now relative stranger. The guy she'd lost her virginity to in one of the inn bedrooms. She reasoned that if you always remembered your first time, he did too. They had that memory shared between them forever.

"Let me know what I can do," Scott told her. "About the inn and about everything else. I'm not great with numbers. You can ask my son. I had to help him with his pre-algebra homework last night, and let's just say, it didn't go well."

Susan's heart sank. But she blinked to look at his ring finger, which was bare. Had he gotten married and divorced? Who had he had a son with? And why was she jealous? She had certainly had her own children and her own life.

"What's his name?" Susan asked.

"Kellan," Scott said.

Susan thought about it for a moment. She wouldn't have picked it, but it seemed modern and interesting. "I like it."

"My wife picked it," he said. "Ex-wife."

They'd already skated too close to important-topic

territory and had only just spoken for a few minutes. Susan guessed this was the sort of intensity that came with what they'd had as teenagers. Susan felt the tug of her best friend's back at the pickup truck and took a delicate step back. Her eyes remained heavy on his.

"Well, they're waiting for me. I'm sorry to rush off like this," she said, pointing a thumb behind her at her girlfriends.

"I get it."

"But I'll see you around, right? You just promised to help with the inn."

Scott nodded. "You'll see me. I always bring the freight and make deliveries to the inn. Me and Chuck, anyway."

"Chuck Frampton. That's a guy I haven't thought about for a while."

In truth, Susan had always disliked Chuck. He was brash and arrogant and did whatever he could to belittle his younger brother and his then-girlfriend, Susan. Anyway, they were all adults now. It didn't matter. She was sure Chuck had grown into an upstanding, genial middle-aged guy as Scott had.

Susan had to force herself to say goodbye again. "I'll see you soon. Enjoy the rest of the night." Then, she rushed back down the staircase, across the stony beach, and back to find Lily and Sarah leaning against the pickup truck with their arms linked together. They beamed at her. She could feel her hair jumping around her, the salt and the air making it all curly and vibrant. When she reached them, she threw her arms around them, totally breathless.

"I just saw Scott Frampton again. I just saw Scott Frampton again." She whispered it like a mantra.

The girls drove back toward the house Susan had grown up in. Sarah shoved an old CD they'd loved from back in the '90s into the CD player—The Cardigans—and the women screamed the lyrics as loud as they could into the warm night air.

"What did he say?" Sarah finally asked, squeezing Susan's elbow hard. "Tell us everything."

Susan's cheeks burned. "I was so stupid, I think."

"Whatever," Lily said. "You're still the same old Susan."

"That's the thing, isn't it? Same *old* Susan."

"Ha. We're all the same age, so I'm taking that as an insult," Sarah said.

"He's still so handsome," Susan told them. She placed her hands on her knees and squeezed hard. She felt overwhelmed as if all the energy she'd gotten from her talk with Scott had brewed up in her stomach and flung itself into every single skin cell. She felt she could run twenty-seven miles. "And he told me he's divorced."

"How did you guys manage to get into such nitty-gritty details in only a few minutes?" Lily asked. Her eyebrow arched, showing her curiosity.

"Come on, Lily, you know how they always were. Intense!" Sarah said with a laugh.

They reached the house just as Susan's phone buzzed in her purse. She tugged it out to read Christine's text.

> Christine: I'll be there tomorrow. The ferry comes into Oak Bluffs at 1:15. Can you pick me up?

"Oh my God," Susan whispered.

"What's up?" Lily asked.

"Christine. She'll be here tomorrow."

"That's fantastic!" Sarah said.

"You don't understand."

"What?" Lily asked.

"We haven't spoken to one another since I left her in New York after a huge fight like five years ago. Maybe six," Susan explained as she chewed on her bottom lip and reread her little sister's text.

Lily and Sarah gave her a wide-eyed look.

"You mean you haven't spoken to Christine at all since then?" Lily asked incredulously.

Susan shook her head slowly, ashamed. "Or Lola."

Both women's jaws dropped. "You're kidding."

"I'm not."

"Wow. You really wanted to get rid of all of this, didn't you?" Lily asked as she spread out her palm and drew a line from one side of the water's horizon to the other, just to the side of the beautiful, weathered house where Susan, Lola, and Christine had grown up.

"I messed up," Susan whispered. "I don't know if I can fix it."

Sarah gave her a knowing look. "Susan Sheridan can fix anything. That's kind of her thing."

Lily looked at Susan as she hopped out of the truck. "Listen, these things happen. Your dad being sick is bringing you all back together. That is all that matters. So embrace it and use the time to heal all the old wounds. You'll be fine, honey!" Lily said and blew Susan a kiss before driving off and leaving her standing there in the driveway. She had a lot to mull over.

Chapter Twelve

S usan felt rejuvenated after her night with her best friends. However, the next morning, as Christine's ferry arrival crept closer and closer, she felt overwhelmed, overburdened, and just plain scared. She walked her dad to the inn in the morning, after yet another carb-bomb croissant, and wandered around town for a while like a lost soul until she grabbed an inn vehicle to pick up Christine. She knew Christine would have some luggage in tow, and there was no way either of them could carry a large suitcase by themselves. In Susan's mind, something was religious about picking something up from the ferry dock, the airport, or even the bus station. *You've come all this way, and all I want to do is greet you the right way.*

Susan remained in the parking lot by the ferry dock for thirty minutes before Christine's arrival. Throughout those minutes, her mind continually returned to the memory of that long-lost day in New York City.

At the time, Christine had been thirty-five years old. That meant Susan had been thirty-eight; Amanda had been sixteen, and Jacob had been nineteen at the time. Susan had been fully entrenched in her career as a criminal lawyer—working side-by-side with Richard to take down some of the gruffest men and women in the Newark area.

To put it plainly, she hadn't exactly been the most empathetic creature on the planet at the time. She'd had two teenagers. A huge career. A husband she tried to please at all times and a huge house with a mortgage to match.

Christine had called her out of the blue. Susan remembered the day particularly well because she'd had a leak in the convertible she had driven at the time. It had rained and stained her brand-new blouse before a very important meeting.

"Hey, Christine. What's up?" This had been the first call Christine had made to Susan in years. But instead of answering hello, she burst into tears. She had howled her name. "Susan! Susan." The pain lurking behind her voice caused Susan to pull over to the nearest gas station to hear her out.

Apparently, Christine had been trying to have a child with her then-boyfriend. They'd been trying for years. "You don't know how expensive IVF is, Susan, but—but I don't even know if it's worth it. It's all this hope and panic and all these shots, and suddenly, you're just told in a little white room that you actually can't have kids, even though that's all you've ever wanted. It's all I've ever wanted, Susan. I wanted to be like Mom! I wanted to have kids the way Mom loved us! I..."

The pain behind her voice caused Susan to immediately rip out of Newark and go to New York. She had called the kids and Richard and told them that she would be out of town for a few nights. She had given Jacob and Amanda money for pizza and had sent off the rest of her work to Richard, telling him it was an emergency. She'd never done anything like that to him before. Of course, he had belittled her for it after she'd returned.

When Susan had found Christine in her New York apartment, she had been inconsolable. She had already drunk herself through an entire bottle of wine and was midway through her second. Her body collapsed forward onto Susan's into a hug, the kind of hug that remembered all past trauma. Susan recalled thinking this was the kind of hug their mother would give Christine. Maybe Christine had thought that too.

Christine's boyfriend had ended things because she had been unable to get pregnant. Susan and Christine spent much of the night drinking and talking. Susan had consoled her and told her it was all right; that although she was going to have an ovary removed, it wasn't the end of the world. She could still have children in a different way if she wanted to. Christine had, of course, taken huge offense at this and said that Susan could never understand. She had thrown a wine bottle at her head.

Still, Susan had stayed on for the next couple of days for support. When Christine had finally gone through with the ovary removal later in the week, Susan had ordered food and cleaned Christine's disgusting Brooklyn apartment, and called a few of her friends to make sure they knew what was going on. Seeing her younger sister stretched out in a hospital bed, recouping from surgery felt so bizarre. Susan knew that there would be a risk that she would never be able to have children, but it was a risk that Christine was willing to take.

Throughout the rest of her stay, Christine had continually turned nasty. Finally, Susan said something about it. "Do you think you can be a little more grateful that I'm here?" she'd asked.

Christine had looked at her with such anger. She had finally yelled at her sister, "Get out of here, Susan. I'm so tired of all your judgment. I'm so tired of you telling me it's all going to be okay when it's obvious I'll never get what I want. We should have known that our lives were ruined for good when Mom died. When Dad did what he did—"

"Are you going to be so childish? Are you going to wallow in your own self-pity?" Susan had returned. Her voice had been cold and calculated.

And it had been the wrong thing to say.

Christine had screamed at Susan so loudly that the nurse came running into her room. Susan recollected leaving—dragging her suitcase down the Brooklyn sidewalk, hailing a cab, and getting a hotel in Manhattan. Manhattan was where she belonged, mentally, at the time. She had gotten a hotel—oh! So this had been the last time she'd gotten a hotel without Richard—and she had stayed up all night crying. She couldn't console Christine, couldn't be the sister she so needed.

Now, she waited for her as the ferry docked. She shuddered, wondering what it would be like to see her again. Christine. Christine Sheridan. Her beautiful sister. The middle child in their forever-broken family.

How could Christine ever forgive her for what she'd done?

And how could any of them really and truly forgive their father?

Christine appeared at the top of the ferry ramp. Her dark brown curls wafted around her shoulders, tousled with the salty air. Immediately, Susan erupted from the car and stood at the side, her gaze glued to Christine. She was dressed in a black dress, cut low over her breasts, and she wore thick New Yorker sunglasses and a stylish blue jean jacket. As she walked, she showed off her thin legs and cast her shoulders back. She looked as though she belonged on a catwalk.

She was a huge contrast to the woman Susan had left in that shoddy apartment in Brooklyn years ago. Only the two of them knew the difference.

Susan walked toward Christine. When Christine noticed her, her own stride faltered. Around them, tourists flooded and poured around them, leaving this strange space in the middle for two sisters to regard each other. After a long pause, Susan stretched her hand toward one of Christine's suitcases. In lieu of hello, she said, "Can I take one?"

Christine handed it off. "Hello to you too."

Susan turned. Together, the two women walked side-by-side, but a million years apart, their chins lifted as they swept toward the car.

"Was your journey okay?" Susan asked. It was still strange that Christine hadn't told her when she would arrive until the day before she had.

"Yes, fine. You know what it's like," Christine said.

"It felt weird, coming back. Like traveling through time," Susan said. She wanted her sister to indulge in this strange feeling with her. Only she and Lola could really feel it the way she had.

But Christine shrugged it off. "Sure. Maybe a little. I don't know." She placed the suitcase into the back of the car, and Susan followed suit with the other one. Susan couldn't help but think that Christine had packed quite a bit for what she had assumed would be a quick trip.

Back in the car, Susan started the engine and eased the car through traffic. Christine coughed and smeared hand lotion over her palms.

"Tourist season again!" Christine sang sarcastically as she looked out the window.

"Weird that it just goes on without us, isn't it?" Susan asked.

"Sure. I don't miss the tourists, though. Look at them. They saved up all their money and counted down the days to come where? Here. The place where we were born. But we didn't ask to be," Christine said.

Susan's heart stirred. She turned her head just a bit. Christine removed her sunglasses to show hazy eyes, proving she'd already had at least one glass of wine. This was the reason for all the brittle words. Christine couldn't handle her temper. Not when she'd had booze.

When they arrived at the house, Susan and Christine placed her suitcases in the bedroom Christine had originally shared with Lola before Susan had left.

"It's like entering a tomb," Christine muttered. She blinked at Lola's Third Eye Blind poster for a long time and scrubbed her fingers through her hair. After she let out a strange laugh, she said, "I don't suppose you'd like a glass of wine, do you?"

Christine and Susan sat on the porch swing overlooking the Nantucket Sound, drinking white wine without speaking. There was too much to say, and it left Susan speechless. Christine's clear anger made her still question why she had come all this way. Maybe it had been a mistake to ask her sisters to come back. Susan was pretty sure she wanted to find the courage to forgive her father, but she couldn't very well demand it from them.

"I just lost my job," Christine suddenly blurted out. She then dropped her head back and sucked down the rest of her glass of wine. She then burst forward, grabbed the bottle, and poured herself another glass.

Susan watched her in stunned silence. Finally, the glass filled again, and she drummed up the courage to say, "I worked at one of the top-rated restaurants on the Upper West Side. We were written up in the *New York Times*, in *Good Eats*, in *Bon Appetit*... Everything you could imagine. There I was as a top-level pastry chef on so many magazine spreads. I felt like I'd finally gotten everything I had ever wanted."

Susan felt her heart dip low. She pressed her lips together, conscious that, as the oldest sister, she always wanted to jump in with advice before it was time.

"Of course, the main guy—Frank—he owned the restaurant. I fell in love with him." Christine lifted a piece of lint from her black dress and flicked it away. "For a few years, we had everything. The fame. The money. The big apartment near Central Park. No, I couldn't give him children—but he already had a toddler with another woman, anyway. The restaurant was our baby.

"Anyway. Frank wasn't so good with money. I had no idea about this, of course. One day, it felt like we were on top of the world. Literally, we had just been on the top of the Eiffel Tower, kissing and telling each other how in love we were. That we could take over the world. And the next day, it seemed like I stood there watching as they said they would dismantle our beautiful restaurant to make way for some sushi spot. I was totally destroyed. We're still together, technically. And there are still a number of things to go over." She swallowed and ripped her hand across her cheek. "This was announced only like a week ago, mind you. I wallowed with Frank for a few days, wondering what would happen with us next, when I thought—what the heck! Guess I'll just come meet the biggest ghost of all. Here, at the pathetic house I grew up in on the Vineyard."

Susan didn't know what to say. She wanted to tell her sister how grateful she was that she'd told her all this. But the moment she opened her lips, her phone buzzed on the table. She frowned at the number and realized it was the Sunrise Cove Inn.

"Sorry..." she muttered as she grabbed the phone. "Hey. This is Susan. What's up?"

It was Natalie. "Susan, I'm so sorry to call you like this, but you really need to come down here. We have something of a situation, and I can't—I just can't calm him down. Your father. You need to get here now."

Chapter Thirteen

Christine made a few sarcastic remarks as they rushed from the house to the inn. "I come all this way, tell you everything about my life, and the next thing I know, you're making me run." Eventually, Susan's panicked expression made Christine close her mouth and carry on. They stumbled a bit when they reached the inn, both of them glossy from the afternoon wine. Christine gripped Susan's elbow—the first physical contact they'd had since she had arrived, and whispered, "My goodness. He really let the thing fall apart, didn't he?"

Susan swallowed. "I don't know what to do about it. If you have any ideas..."

"This was his life. He gave everything to this place. He would have traded any one of his daughters and even his wife for this place. And now look at it. It's a dump."

Susan cast Christine a dark look and cleared her throat. "Let's just go see what's going on."

Christine and Susan entered the inn to find Wes Sheridan more irate than Susan had seen him since they'd been girls. He stood, holding some kind of clipboard in front of what appeared to be a husband and wife in their mid-thirties and their three young children, all of whom blinked up at Wes, terribly frightened.

"I've told you, again and again, you only booked for one week!" Wes cried. "It's right here in the books."

"Mr. Sheridan, please understand. We talked on the phone months ago. I told you we needed to be at Martha's Vineyard for two weeks. You echoed it back to me, 'Two weeks!' And you told me you would give me it at a reduced price. Remember?" The husband shifted his weight and glared at Susan's father. "And now, you tell me this morning that we have to leave our room one week early... And you don't have another room in your inn for us."

"You only booked one week. I know this for sure. I wouldn't make a mistake like that. I've worked at this inn since I was a little boy," Wes insisted. "Younger than these kids, even."

Susan leaped up to stand next to her father. She gave the family a big smile, hoping to quell the anger and tension in the room. Natalie still stood behind the front desk, rubbing her palms together anxiously.

"What seems to be the problem, then?" Susan asked.

The father arched his brow. "And who might you be?"

"I'm an associate of the inn. Susan Harris. So glad you decided to stay with us here at the inn."

"Yes. Well. It was terribly pleasant until this very moment. Mr. Sheridan here doesn't have another room for us, and we checked in the rest of Oak Bluffs and Edgartown. It's all booked up," the man explained his situation. He rubbed at his sweaty neck while one of his young children grabbed his hand and tugged at it hard.

"I see." Susan clucked her tongue. "I really am sorry. Mistakes do happen. I hope you can understand that."

What was it about the hospitality business that enraged people so much? Susan had worked as a criminal lawyer, and still, she had never seen people more riled up than when they were tourists who hadn't gotten their way.

Granted, this was a bit more complicated.

"If you don't have anything to offer us, I don't know what we're going to do," the man said. His voice rose, probably due to his child tugging at him so hard.

Susan swallowed and turned to her dad. "Mr. Sheridan, do you think you could head to your office and wait for me there? Now."

Her father's nostrils flared. He wasn't the sort of man to welcome being told what to do. But he was angry and volatile, and nobody needed his continued help in this situation. He nodded and cut back toward the office. When he was out of earshot, the father scoffed, "Thank you for getting him out of here."

Susan cast him a dark look as she turned toward Natalie. "So, you're telling me that there's not another room?"

Natalie shook her head, her eyes wide. "There is nothing available. And there's really nothing I can do at this moment. I-I don't even think I was around when Wes booked them. I took a few weeks off around then, and..."

Suddenly, a voice boomed out from the hallway that led to the bistro. "What seems to be the trouble?"

Susan turned to find Scott Frampton all decked out in what seemed to be his freight clothes: dark green shorts and a dark green shirt, his face tanned and handsome, with a perfect five o'clock shadow across his cheeks.

The father of the family seemed overly willing to declare what had happened to him to any onlooker. He blurted, "They overbooked the inn and are leaving us out in the cold."

Scott arched his brow. "Well, first of all, I hope you understand that the people of the Sunrise Cove Inn would never leave you out in the cold."

Susan felt Christine's enormous eyes on her. She gave a slight shrug as Scott took the last few strides across the rest of the lobby floor and shook the husband's and wife's hands.

"You've stayed here for how long?" Scott asked.

"A week," the man answered.

"But you seem pretty angry. I wouldn't think a week on Martha's Vineyard should make anyone as upset as you are right now," Scott said with a smile.

This was Scott's way. He could always calm any situation. Across the lobby, Christine mouthed the words, *Is that Scott Frampton?* Her gaze remained locked on Scott.

"It's just we don't know what to do," the husband said.

"Well, you've checked the other hotels and inns on the island, haven't you?" Scott said.

The husband gave a lopsided shrug. "At least for tonight. They're all booked."

"And what about tomorrow?" Scott asked. "Any sign about that?"

The father collected his phone and clicked for a second or two. "I guess there are a few rooms available in Edgartown tomorrow through the rest of our stay."

"That's fantastic news!" Scott said. "And in the meantime, I guess there's only one option for what you should do next."

"What? Sleep on the beach?" the father asked.

"Absolutely not. You'll stay at my place," Scott affirmed.

Christine's jaw dropped even lower. Susan's heart leaped. The husband looked as though he was prepared to say no, but the wife grabbed his elbow and whispered something in his ear. The husband grumbled, "If it really isn't putting you out."

"Not at all," Scott said. "I can't imagine a better way to use the place. Now, it isn't Buckingham Palace, that's for sure, but it is my home. It's clean, and it has its own little beach and dock for the kids to play in the water. I'll let you stay there for free for all your trouble. Do you mind?"

The husband looked defeated. His shoulders sloped forward as he extended his hand forward to shake Scott's in gratitude.

"Thank you," he said. "I really do appreciate this. I'll book the other hotel in Edgartown right now."

The family scuttled off toward the bistro to finalize their booking. When they disappeared, Natalie jumped up and down and smacked her hands together. She looked close to tears.

"Scott! I didn't know how we would get our way out of that one!" she cried.

Scott beamed at Susan and tilted his head. Susan laughed. "You look like you're up to something."

"Nah. It's just—didn't I tell you that I would help you out?"

"Didn't think it would come so quickly. Thank you," Susan said. A flush spread across her cheeks.

"Scott! I bet you don't remember me," Christine said. Her voice was brighter than it had been, almost false. She hugged Scott—something she had very noticeably and purposefully not done with her sister.

"Christine, wow! It's good to see you again," Scott said. The hug broke, and he beamed at both of them. "Wow. Two of the three sisters were back together again. What will happen when you get Lola back here?"

"The whole world will catch fire, probably," Christine said, laughing. "Of course, it seems like we have bigger fish to fry at the moment. You just gave up your house for the night."

Scott shrugged. "Oh, it doesn't matter. I can always stay with Chuck if I need to."

"Nonsense! You should stay with us," Christine said. "We have space on either the pull-out couch or that other bedroom if Susan sleeps with me. You really must. You saved us."

Susan knew Christine was up to something. However, what she had suggested was kind and generous, and everything Susan might have done had she been able to think clearly with Scott around.

Scott rubbed the back of his neck contemplatively. "Chuck and I just have a few more rounds to make, and then, I guess, I can stop by. Yes. Of course. I'd love to."

"Yes! Fantastic. That means we're having a little party," Christine said. Her smile grew wider. "Guess me and Susie will have to go shopping."

"Anything you girls cook will be fantastic, I bet," Scott said. "Although I have to say, anything would be better than what you used to cook me back in the day. That weird cheddar lasagna you made up."

"Hey! It was cheese and noodles. What else do you want?" Susan asked with a laugh.

Scott said goodbye and hustled back to the truck with Chuck. Christine and Susan blinked at each other, a standoff in the middle of the inn lounge.

"What are you up to?" Susan asked.

"I guess I should ask you the same thing," Christine said.

"I ran into Scott last night. That's all. He offered to help out with the inn," Susan returned.

"I feel like there's electricity in here. I can feel the spark myself, big sis," Christine said.

On the other side of the front desk, Natalie nodded in agreement with a large smile splayed on her lips.

"I mean, we used to be in love like a thousand years ago, it feels like. Of course, there would be something," Susan said.

Why did Christine have to make everything so poisonous?

"Besides. I am a divorced woman," Susan blurted then.

Christine looked as if all the wind had been knocked out of her. Susan's nostrils flared as she whipped her left hand into the air to show off her naked finger.

"Not that you actually care what's going on in my life. Not that you'd ever call and say hi," she exclaimed.

"Like I would want to call you after our last sister session in New York," Christine threw back.

Natalie pretended to take a phone call in the next room. Christine and Susan faced off for a long moment. Susan felt she might burst into tears or laughter—she wasn't sure which.

With a jolt, Susan remembered her father in the

office. She rushed toward it, with Christine hot on her heels.

"Don't run away from me! You can't just..."

Susan stopped short at the office to find her father up near the stereo system. He played an old song he'd loved ever since Susan was a kid, a track from the early '80s. He tapped his feet along with the music and swayed. When he spotted Christine and Susan in the doorway, he pointed at the speaker and said, "I love this song!"

Susan smiled. "It's really good. Really good. Dad—I just wanted to tell you that we got everything worked out with the family in the lobby. It's all fine."

Her dad kept tapping his feet. He turned around fast and flashed his hands out, and wiggled his fingers. His grin widened. It was obvious that he had no idea what she was talking about. He had already forgotten.

"Dad...?" Christine asked.

"Christine! Oh, my God," he said, taking a step closer. He wrapped her in a bear hug as Susan stood back and watched them. Her heart swelled at the moment. Finally, they released each other.

"Hi, Dad. You look really good!" Christine said, smiling.

"You look beautiful, honey. It's been so long," he said as he looked at both of his daughters.

"Yes, it has been, but I'm here now, and I'll be staying for a few days so we can catch up. All right?" Christine said. She watched as her father shook his head in understanding.

"Dad, we're going to run to the store and pick up some supplies. You'll be okay here, right? Let Natalie know if you need anything," Susan said.

Slowly, the girls backed out of the room. When they

reached the hallway, Christine fell forward into Susan's arms. This was the first hug they had shared. Christine shook as she poured her forehead into Susan's shoulder. The weeping came next. Susan slid her hand across Christine's back and whispered, "It's going to be all right. We're all going to be back together again. We're going to find a way to be okay."

Chapter Fourteen

S usan watched Christine carefully as they walked toward the little supermarket on the corner. Christine kept her head down, and her shoulders rolled forward, no longer looking like the stoic and beautiful New Yorker who had arrived on the ferry earlier that day.

The market was totally updated from the last time either of them had been there. Back in the old days, there had been a little ice cream and coffee area at the front, with little diner-like tables and chairs with a beautiful view of the street for people watching. Now, the store had grown bigger, and they'd blotted out the little ice cream area for a variety of beer and wine. Without speaking, Christine headed toward the wine section and placed several bottles into a basket that hung off her elbow. When she turned to see Susan's incredulous look, she shrugged and said, "We're going to have loads of people over for dinner tonight. They're going to want to drink."

Susan knew she was right. She grabbed a cart of her own and added crates of beer before heading into the deeper sections of the store to get meat for burgers, slices of cheese, burger buns, bags of chips, watermelon, and potato salad. It wasn't the kind of thing she would have made her family back at home--at least, not in the past few years--but it was the kind of fare she'd grown up with. She knew her family would find comfort in it.

Christine and Susan checked out. Christine half reached for her purse, but Susan waved. "I've got it." They collected the bags at the end of the checkout line and then headed back into the sun. With all the bottles of wine and crates of beer, Susan knew they would need some kind of vehicle.

"Do you mind if I just run back to the inn and grab another car?" she asked.

Christine looked disgruntled. "What if someone sees me out here?"

"Who is going to see you?"

"I don't know. The entire town is a gossip trap," Christine returned.

"I'm pretty sure people knew you were coming because of Dad," Susan said. "And the entire island didn't stop because of it. Look." She nodded toward the glittering downtown of Oak Bluffs, swirling with tourists and locals alike, all with light smiles and bright eyes.

"Fine," Christine grumbled. "Just hurry."

Susan was back in five minutes. Christine reported that only one person had spotted her and recognized her. "My English teacher, Mrs. Robinson—who looks fantastic, by the way. It's really like time stopped for her. I'm so jealous."

"Oh! I forgot about her," Susan said. She cranked the engine and turned the car toward the parking lot exit. As they drove, however, Zach Walters burst out from the sidewalk and waved. He wore his chef uniform, without the hat, and his blue eyes were bright and warm.

"Is that..." Christine muttered ominously.

Susan yanked down the window. "Hey, Zach! What's up?"

Zach leaned down to speak through the window. "Hey, Susie! I had to run to the store to grab a few extra ingredients. I heard there was a bit of chaos in the lobby earlier."

"You could say that," Susan said. "Hey. You remember my sister, don't you? Christine?"

Susan flashed her eyes toward Christine to find her stone-faced, her eyes glittering angrily. It was clear that she hadn't forgotten or forgiven poor Zach for whatever he had done back to her in high school.

"Christine Sheridan. I'd recognize you anywhere," Zach said. His voice seemed strangely sarcastic to Susan, as though he wanted to toy with her as much as he could.

"Zach Walters. To what do I owe this unique pleasure?"

Zach chuckled. "I work for the Sunrise Cove Inn! In the bistro."

Christine kept her voice level, but it still held a sarcastic edge to it. "Oh, lucky us. Since when?"

"Since late last summer. It's been a remarkable thing working there with your father. The work is hard, but I have a lot of experience working in Boston, and this definitely has a lighter feel to it. Say, weren't you working in New York City? I heard that you were a pastry chef in a pretty famous restaurant. Upper West Side, right?"

"Yes. We're quite successful," Christine shot back.

"And the restaurant owner? I think I read something about him. He's your boyfriend?"

"That's right," Christine said. "We're pretty happy with it. It's our dream."

"I'm so glad you got everything you ever wanted," Zach returned.

"And I'm so glad you got to come back to the island. It's where you belong," Christine said.

Susan interjected, sensing a battle was about to be waged, "Okay! Well. I guess we had better head off to our house. We're having a little family get-together tonight. At least, I think we are. I still have to invite everyone."

"Well, enjoy yourselves. Welcome back to the island, Christine. I hope I can pick your ear about that restaurant soon. Maybe you can share your secrets of the trade," Zach said before he rapped the top of the car to send them on their way.

"Absolute idiot," Christine muttered as Susan eased out of the parking lot. "I bet he knows the restaurant went under, and he just wants to rub my face in it."

"Why was it you two never got along? I can't for the life of me remember," Susan said, her brow furrowed.

"It doesn't matter. Just get me home. I need a drink."

* * *

Back at the house, Susan invited mostly her family, which included Aunt Kerry, Uncle Trevor, their children, Charlotte, Claire, Steven, and Kelli, along with all their spouses and children. When she added herself, Scott, Christine, and her father to the list, the number seemed so big to her. She had given up on the homemaker role years ago but now had to find it within herself again. She fired up the grill and set to work while Christine sliced up vegetables and watermelon and arranged burger buns on the picnic table on the porch overlooking the Sound. Both drank as they went—Christine lapping Susan pretty quickly after they began. But their conversation also flowed easily. They danced around topics of their mother, marveled at what it meant to be back at this old house after so long, and discussed what they currently knew about Lola. It wasn't much.

"It really is a mess around here," Susan said as she formed the burger into patties. "Dad never got rid of anything. The house is a museum."

"It's our project for the next few weeks, isn't it?" Christine asked with an eyebrow arched.

"Well, if it isn't too much trouble. I know you probably want to get back to Frank," Susan said as she rinsed her hands in the sink.

Christine grumbled something Susan couldn't really hear. When she turned her head up to ask, the door inside the house sprung open. Aunt Kerry's voice hollered, "Is there a Christine Sheridan in this house?"

Despite her clear rage at the world, Christine looked overwhelmed with excitement to see her aunt again. She flung her arms around the beautiful older woman—admittedly the only mother figure the girls had after losing Anna. Aunt Kerry cuddled her close, then reared back. "Let me get a look at you. My goodness. You look every bit the New Yorker you've become."

Christine blushed. "Don't be silly. I look like a ragamuffin."

"Not for a minute. You know, I read all about that restaurant you and that very handsome man run up on the Upper West Side. I always tell Trevor we should take a trip up there, but you know, he's no city guy."

Very quickly, everyone appeared for dinner. Natalie

drove Wes back from the inn and joined them. Susan blinked around at these vibrant faces: from Aunt Kerry and Uncle Trevor to cousin Steven and his wife Laura and their children Isabella and Jonathon—who came with his two babies and young wife, Carrie. Cousin Kelli brought her husband, Mike, a real estate broker on the island, who'd largely taken over much of Aunt Kerry and Uncle Trevor's clientele. They brought their children, Sam, twenty-one, Josh, nineteen, and Lexi, who was seventeen. Then there was Charlotte and her daughter, Rachel, and Claire, her twin girls, Abby and Gail, and her husband, Russel.

The porch spilled out onto the front lawn, where Claire's husband, Russel, set up another few tables for everyone. Luckily, Cousin Kelli had suspected that Susan hadn't accounted for everyone's hunger and had brought loads more burgers, burger buns, bags of chips, and even more crates of beer. One of the family's younger members, Josh, set to work on a playlist that he blared from a portable speaker placed on the porch's corner. The songs were perfect hits from long-lost summers.

"My goodness," Christine said when she managed to sneak away from another conversation to find Susan in the kitchen. "I have to say. I have not thought about a lot of these people in years."

"I know. But they have totally opened their arms to us," Susan murmured. "I can't tell if it makes me feel guilty or overwhelmed or sad or happy or everything at once."

"Did you know about Jason, Charlotte's husband?" Christine asked, her brow furrowed.

"Died in a fishing accident. Yeah. I only just learned about it," Susan affirmed.

"So sad," Christine said softly.

Both of them felt the echoes of the past. The death of their mother and the sadness of it etched across Jason's young daughter, Rachel.

"At least we had each other," Christine said suddenly, surprising Susan.

Before Susan could respond, Scott's familiar boom of a voice came in from the back hallway. He appeared seconds later. He had changed into a pair of jeans and a button-down shirt, and he'd showered and added a touch of cologne. He beamed at Susan, and Susan felt uneasy on her legs. She leaned hard against the kitchen counter and felt an enormous smile form.

"Hey there!" she said, looking up at him.

He lifted a crate of beer. "I know it's impolite to ever come to something like this empty-handed. I didn't imagine that you'd invited the entire island to your house, though."

"Things got a little out of hand," Christine agreed.

"The more, the merrier!" Scott said. He stepped toward Susan and leaned forward a bit. For a moment, Susan had the rushing, panicked thought that he might kiss her right there in front of everyone. But of course, all he wanted was a hug. She gave it, her motions awkward, and her head was spinning.

"Here. I'll take the beer," Susan said. She needed to do something with herself before she fell against him and hugged him tighter against her.

She wasn't a weak-minded woman who needed a man like that.

Finally, everyone sat at around the same time for the feast. Susan sat at one of the main porch tables with Scott, her father, Aunt Kerry, Christine, and Claire. Together, they piled up their burgers and swapped stories of their day. Generally, Christine and Susan hung back a bit, letting everyone else talk since they were outsiders and had to learn the rules of the Vineyard world or, better yet, get back up to speed. It was always just like riding a bike again. Soon, though, both girls were doubled over in laughter at the silly banter and jokes that everyone flew around easily.

Namely, Susan was surprised at how hilarious Scott was. She felt overly drawn to him, her eyes catching his in the middle of his stories. Maybe it was because of this distraction that Susan didn't notice that Christine had poured nearly an entire bottle of wine to herself since the start of dinner.

"You remember it, don't you, Susan?" Wes began. He placed his half-eaten burger on his plate and rubbed his palms together. "Your mother and I were trying to teach you how to ride a bicycle. We were on this road out back, and you were so determined. I'd never seen anyone as determined as a young Susan Sheridan. Anyway, out of nowhere, this huge cow emerged from the forest. A farm cow! The girl scared our Susan so badly that she tumbled off the bike and scraped her knees to high heaven. She refused to get on the bike again for at least a week."

Susan belly-laughed. She did remember that, albeit vaguely. Wes reached across the table and gripped her hand hard. He drew his other arm around Christine's shoulders. "I'm just so glad to have my two girls here. So, so glad."

Christine's face drained of color. She shot up from the table in a split second, nearly toppling paper plates to the ground. She sniffed. "I just have to run upstairs for a second."

Susan followed after her. When they reached the staircase, Christine almost stumbled over with her drunkenness. Susan could hardly believe her eyes. Christine collapsed on her childhood bed upstairs, and her body shook while Susan stood over her, waiting.

"What did he say? What happened?" Susan whispered. In her mind, everything had gone smoothly until then. It had all seemed okay.

"He just. He can pretend so easily that nothing bad ever happened," Christine blurted. She drew her head up to show her blotchy cheeks and red eyes. "Telling these stupid old nostalgic stories. As though he didn't..." She broke into tears again. "I just don't know how you can forgive him like this, Susan. I don't know why you dragged me here. It's too much to deal with."

"Christine... Dad is sick. Really sick. You saw him earlier today."

Christine let out another cry. Susan sighed. She couldn't reason with her. Not today. She rose and headed back to the hallway, back to her huge and vibrant family. Christine needed time. And maybe it was already too late for her to come back.

Chapter Fifteen

Scott left the Sheridan house early in the morning, around four forty-five. Sneaking out the back door reminded him of the few times he had sneaked into Susan's bedroom in high school, slept over as long as he could, and then headed back to his house in the dead of night. He would have done anything to be close to her back then. Now didn't seem so different.

It had been a really remarkable night. He had been allowed to sit next to Susan for most of it. She still smelled the same: like lilacs and honey, and her laugh rang out at all the ridiculous and silly things he said as though they were much cleverer. Wes Sheridan had been in good spirits, and even Christine had been okay until she had disappeared. Susan had whispered only that Christine was very tired from her trip to the Vineyard. Her eyes had told another story.

Scott met up with Chuck at around five to head off to the mainland to pick up the supplies for the day. They were both bleary-eyed, gazing out across the hazy fog of the Sound as they sipped burnt cups of coffee.

"Still can't believe you gave over your house to those tourists," Chuck coughed.

Scott shrugged. "It was a good night at the Sheridan's. I have no complaints at all. I just told the tourists to leave the keys in the mailbox."

"Right. Like it would ever be hard to break into that tiny house." Chuck scoffed.

"Ha," Scott said.

"You just want as much time with your old fling as you can get," Chuck said, mocking him. "Just remember that she isn't a Vineyard girl anymore. She's lived a whole life away from here. She'll want to go back to that."

Scott didn't answer. He knew, on some level, that Chuck was probably right. Still, he loved living in this impossible reality.

They finished their rounds just after one in the afternoon. Chuck headed off to have a beer with an old friend, while Scott changed his clothes again, added a dab of cologne, and then walked over to the Sunrise Cove Inn. He had said he wanted to help Susan with the repairs and felt more energy than he had in years. Today seemed like the perfect day to start.

To his surprise, when he walked in through the front door, he found Susan at the front desk rather than Natalie or Wes. Susan wore a beautiful lavender dress and a pair of gold hooped earrings, and when she lifted her head to say, "Welcome to Sunrise Cove Inn," she was beautiful in every sense, the sort of person you would want to greet you when you entered into a place like that. Of course, when she realized that Scott was Scott, she blushed and said, "Oh, I'm sorry. I'm not really used to this job yet. I hope I didn't sound too silly."

"Not at all," Scott said.

"What brings you to the inn?"

"I just finished up with my daily rounds and wondered if you needed any of that help we talked about. Maybe some paint? The shutters outside that are hanging a bit crooked? Anything like that?"

Susan beamed. "Wow. Are you telling me that a man actually plans to stick to his word? Should I alert the local news?"

"No interviews, please," Scott said. His smile spread from cheek to cheek.

"Great. Well, you know where the shed is in the back, right? There are plenty of tools in there. As far as paint goes, I have the sample here. It matches what we need exactly. If you want, you can run to the hardware store and use the inn credit card. Here..." She placed the plastic card into his hands.

"That is a lot of responsibility," he said and flashed her a wink.

"Do you think you can handle it?"

"I hope so."

"Otherwise, you know I'll come after you. I know where you live," Susan said, giggling.

"Nothing could save me from the wrath of Susan Sheridan," Scott replied and then slapped the counter before he turned away.

Scott got to work. He headed to the hardware store with the paint sample and the credit card and loaded up his truck with new shutters, paint, and paintbrushes. As he drove back, he caught himself whistling several times. He couldn't believe it: he was headed back to help Susan Sheridan with the Sunrise Cove Inn. If he was honest with himself, this had also been part of the original dream. He'd wanted him and Susan to take over the inn after her parents retired. He had imagined helping Anna and Wes as they grew older, the way Wes and Anna had with Wes's parents.

Gosh. He hadn't remembered that fantasy in a long, long time.

The afternoon drifted into the evening as Scott cleaned the inn's exterior and removed the broken shutters. A middle-aged couple approached him in the middle and said, "We've been coming to the Sunrise Cove Inn for years. So glad you're finally fixing it up. It's our favorite place, and it's made us sad to see it fall into disrepair like this."

"We're so glad you always choose Sunrise Cove Inn," Scott told them with a smile. "It's a family place. It's been in business since the forties. All it needs is a little tender lovin' care."

Just after six, Scott entered the lobby again to check on Susan. She was bent over the ledgers, her brow furrowed as she clicked through a calculator and muttered to herself. Scott swiped his hand across his forehead; he'd sweated himself silly over the past few hours.

"What the heck..." Susan whispered.

"What seems to be the problem?" Scott asked, his brows furrowed together.

Susan's almond-shaped eyes flashed up to find him standing there watching her. "Oh. I don't know. I'm probably just really bad at math. I wanted to enter what you had purchased today for the repairs, but when I looked at the ledgers a little bit more, it seems like we've lost much more money than my dad thinks. Maybe that's the reason he's avoided repairing this place altogether. I just can't figure out where it went."

Scott glanced at the ledger. It was all a jumbled-up

list of numbers and calendar dates and signatures. Before he could get a second look, she snapped it closed and sighed. "I don't know. I can't look at it anymore. I've been adding and subtracting for the past two hours. My head might explode." Slowly, a smile inched across her face. "Plus, I'm completely famished. And you must be too."

"You know me too well," Scott said. Immediately, he winced. There was too much truth in what he said.

But Susan didn't point this out. She tapped over to the side doorway, which led to another collection of offices. "Natalie? Are you ready to clock in? I'm going to step away for the night."

Scott entered the staff lounge to scrub up and change his shirt. When he emerged, Susan waited for him and led him into the bistro. It was about three-quarters full, with tourists and locals from all over gabbing with delight over their salads, steaks, lobster, and other buttery seafood. They went naturally to the table Susan's father liked the best.

"If Dad knows anything, it's how to pick a good view," Susan said as Scott drew the chair back for her to sit. She blushed and added, "I don't remember the last time someone has done that for me. Thank you."

Scott and Susan both ordered starter salads and Atlantic salmon. After a bit of hesitation, Scott ordered them a bottle of Riesling. He told himself not to bring up Christine's reckless drinking the night before. Everyone had noticed; everyone had been worried. Nobody had known what to do.

"You've had a crazy few days, haven't you?" he said after their glasses had been poured and they'd settled in.

Susan gave him a wide-eyed look. "It's been like a hurricane. One minute, I'm a criminal lawyer in Newark. Besides the clients, who always changed, I was sure my life had already been hashed out. I had the perfect house, the perfect husband, and the perfect children. And then one day—poof! I realized that nothing in Newark belonged to me anymore. Around that time, Aunt Kerry called, and... now, well. Now I'm grilling burgers and adding up Sunrise Cove Inn ledgers."

"Both suit you," Scott said truthfully. He sipped his wine contemplatively. How was she more beautiful than she had been twenty-five years before?

"That's kind. I don't know. Actually, the only thing keeping me sane at the moment is moving as quickly as possible to clean everything up. Your help today with the inn was stupendous."

"I'm not done yet," Scott affirmed. "I'll be back every day until it's done."

"You really don't have to do that," Susan said. "Once we figure out the money situation, I'll hire someone properly."

"It's not like I have anything else keeping me at home," Scott returned.

Silence fell across the table. Scott regretted his words despite their truthfulness. Maybe it was time for him to add a bit more to the picture she had of him.

"I do talk to my son on the phone every other day," he said. "He's a good kid. Really creative. Quiet. Maybe a little too quiet. But I like to think he just doesn't want to step in it, the way I always did as a teenager."

Susan chuckled. "You were a bit brash sometimes."

"That's putting it kindly. There were only two things I knew back then. One that I knew everything there was to know. And two, I loved you more than life itself, Susan

Sheridan. I've thought about it a great deal over the years."

Susan dropped her eyes to the glow of the white table-cloth. Again, the silence stretched between them.

"There I go again. Stepping in it," Scott said, leaning back against his chair.

This made Susan laugh again. His heart stopped its wild beating and returned to normal. Their salmon arrived, and they were allowed conversation topics that weren't so gut-wrenchingly painful. Still, he was grateful for every minute that ticked by because he was allowed to share them with her.

Chapter Sixteen

Since the fight with Christine after the barbecue, Christine had kept a large berth from Susan. When Susan walked past her bedroom, she heard her in conversation with someone on the phone. The conversations were tense and mean-spirited, at least on Christine's side. Susan had to assume that they were with Frank. Like all Christine's relationships, this seemed to be a ticking time bomb. It hurt Susan's heart—but it also lined up with every single thing she knew about her sister. Christine had never been one to stick to someone for long. In high school, she'd danced through boys easily, forcing them to chase after her and beg for her until she dumped them and allowed it all to happen again.

Now, at the age of forty-one, with just the one ovary, a dramatic history of drinking, a closed-up restaurant, and no job, Christine seemed to be at the end of her rope.

There was still no word from Lola. Susan hustled out onto the porch and winced in pain. She perched at the edge of the porch swing and flipped through her purse to find her weed pen and phone.

Susan: Lola, hey. I haven't heard from you. Just wondering if we can expect you in the next few days? We want to go through Mom's stuff and clean up the house a little bit. Christine is here, and the Vineyard is prettier than ever.

When she finished the text, she sighed, closed her eyes, took several hits from the weed pen, and dropped her head back, falling into the goodness. The cloud of no-feeling fell over her. She felt all light as the pain slowly subsided. It was as if her body started to become numb all over.

And then, the porch door creaked open. Christine's voice sprung out. "What are you smoking?"

Susan was far away for a second. She dragged herself back and opened her eyes to find Christine hovering over her, her hand wrapped around a glass of wine and her eyes in their own state of fogginess.

"It's nothing," Susan sputtered. She dropped the pen into her purse and righted herself, tending to her hair. She was a bit too high to care about what happened, but she didn't need Christine to learn everything. Not like this.

Christine chuckled and dropped onto the swing. "You were always such a Goody Two-shoes. It's hard for me to believe that you've dipped yourself into the world of herb."

"World of herb? Listen to yourself," Susan said, laughing. Actually, she laughed a little too hard.

"Suit yourself, girl. I have never been one for weed. Not since college, which, you might remember, I dropped out of. Largely because I liked the green stuff a little too much. No, I'll stick to wine, thank you. No sharing required," Christine said.

Weirdly, it seemed that Christine discovering this small part of Susan's secret had built a doorway for them to speak through again.

"Is Dad still at the inn?" Christine asked.

"Yes. Till six," Susan said.

"He's a little too sick to work there during the day, don't you think?"

"Maybe. Not yet. He loves it so much. I can't imagine telling him to leave for good. We're a small staff at this point, so we need him occasionally at the desk."

"Listen to yourself. Using the word 'we'. You've included yourself on the staff roster, free of pay, I guess," Christine said.

Susan shrugged. "I told you. I don't have anything else. I feel like I owe it to Dad. Or if not to Dad, to Mom."

Christine's mischievous smile fell. She tipped herself forward to make the porch swing sway. "I haven't missed her as much as I do right now in years. Sometimes, I will be walking down the street in New York, and I'll just have the weirdest idea that I want to call her. It's crazy because I don't remember calling her much when she was alive. She was always just a few rooms or a few streets away. And I don't even know what we would talk about now. She lived her entire life on the island. She married our dad when she was very young and started having kids immediately. Bang. Bang. Bang. The way you did."

"Ha. True," Susan murmured.

"I wish I would have. Gosh, I just... There was so much I didn't know about myself. And now, it's all too late."

Susan and Christine didn't speak for a long time. Out on the water, Stan Ellis shot his little boat across the blue to find a perfect fishing spot. Susan had seen him nearly every day since that first one, but never on land.

"I think Dad misses her too. Mom. He brings her up as much as possible," Susan said.

"That doesn't change what he did," Christine returned.

"I just think, if we don't find a way to forgive him before he... before it's too late, we're going to regret it for the rest of our lives," Susan said. "I know that sounds dramatic and stupid to you. I know you haven't wanted to think about our family for a long time. But it's fact."

Suddenly, there was a dramatic crash from inside the house. Susan and Christine rose to see the door that led to the driveway wide open to reveal a picture-perfect angel, the woman of their forever dreams. There, standing in the doorway, was their mother: Anna Sheridan.

"Are those my girls?" the voice cried out.

"Lola," Susan murmured as her hand covered her mouth in surprise. She rushed through the door from the porch to view her gorgeous youngest sister: thirty-eight years old, fresh out of Boston as a journalist with the entire world at her feet. She was dressed in bohemian fashion and incredibly trim, and her eyes glowing with excitement. Although Susan hadn't seen her youngest sister in years, it was entirely Lola-esque to surprise them rather than tell them when she planned to arrive.

Immediately, the girls threw their arms around each other. The three Sheridan sisters had come together for the first time in twenty-five years. Tears trickled down Susan's cheeks. When she drew back, she noticed that tears had struck each and every one of them.

"You kept it from us!" Christine cried. "I can't believe you."

Lola grinned wider. "You know how I love an entrance."

The three sisters returned to the porch. Christine opened another bottle of wine. The conversation both bubbled and broke, depending on the moment. Sometimes, all they could do was gaze at one another in disbelief. Again, Susan felt herself dwell in sadness. She had seen Lola for only a few hours at dinner a few years ago, but beyond that, Susan had left the island when Lola was only around twelve or thirteen. Lola had had to remain on Martha's Vineyard without their mother for years, constantly surrounded by old and painful memories.

Maybe this was part of the reason Susan had always felt extra guilty about Lola. She should have stuck around, if only for her. She'd had to fend for herself.

"I brought presents!" Lola cried suddenly. She whipped out her artsy-looking, bespoke purse and found three little jewelry boxes. She passed two of them to Christine and Susan, who opened them to find little unique stones hanging from leather necklaces. Lola said that she had just done an interview with a local artist coming up in the Boston art scene, who'd given her the necklaces at a really good rate.

Nothing about the necklace screamed, "forty-four-year-old mother of two and grandmother of two, without a husband and with no real hope for the future," but that almost made Susan love it all the more. She hugged Lola tight and thanked her.

After that, Christine and Susan tried to update Lola on the situation at the inn.

"So Dad's really lost it, huh?" Lola said. She sounded kind of flippant about it, as though Wes Sheridan was just someone she'd heard of a few times rather than the father she had spent a lot of time in that house alone with.

"He's losing bits of pieces of himself all the time," Susan affirmed. "But I've decided to stay here at the inn until we decide what to do. Maybe, who knows, we sell it? I don't know."

Both Christine and Lola sat with this. Susan had hardly admitted this to herself. But when she really looked at the reality of the situation, what other choice might they have?

"I don't know. Mom put so much of herself into that place. I just..." Lola stuttered for a second, lost in thought. She then drew a fist and smashed it on her knee. "I don't know! Man, this is the hardest thing in the world, isn't it? But look at this island. Look at this place we grew up in! I try to describe it to people. That we had a little hideaway from the rest of the world, but you really can't envision it until you're encircled by it."

Just before six, Susan announced that Wes would be home soon. Lola's face changed. She and Christine made heavy eye contact and returned their gaze to Susan.

"I just don't know if I'm fully ready to see Dad right now," Lola said. "I couldn't wait to see you two, but a night with Dad?"

"He's really a lot more gentle than you're giving him credit," Susan said. "He just wants his family to be together."

"It's just been such a long time. So much pain," Lola said. "I don't know if I can face him and pretend everything is okay."

"But we're all here, Lola." Susan felt anger and adrenaline swirl in her stomach. "He could be gone soon. We have to make peace. We have to face this. Otherwise..."

But they heard the door crank open near the driveway before she could finish. Wes Sheridan, the father of the three Sheridan sisters, now home for the first time together in twenty-five years, called out, "Girls? I'm home!" Just as he'd done years and years before.

Lola's eyes became huge, like saucers. She then exhaled the breath she had been holding. "All right. Let's do this. I guess there's no turning back now."

Chapter Seventeen

The three Sheridan sisters walked into the house together: Susan first, Christine second, and Lola third. A stooped and older version of their father awaited them at the kitchen counter: no longer the dominant and loud and powerful man who'd screamed at them as young children and teenagers. He placed the inn keys on the countertop with a clank. His eyes seemed absolutely glued to Lola. Again, Susan was struck with the knowledge that Lola was the spitting image of their mother, Anna.

And now—she remembered: Lola was the same age Anna had been when she died. She was thirty-eight years old.

Lola could sense what this had done to their father. She took a small step forward and said, probably to save herself from his assertion that she was Anna, his Anna, "Hi, Dad. It's me. Lorraine. Lola."

Their father's eyes weathered a few moments of confusion before coming into the present. "Lola. Wow. You came! I didn't think you would."

Susan breathed a sigh of relief. Tentatively, Lola stepped forward with her arms on either side of her and fell into a hug. Wes closed his eyes and inhaled slowly. When Lola drew back again, Wes marveled, "I can't believe it. All my girls are in the house."

It was decided that they would order pizza. There wasn't time to cook, not with all the catching up the four of them had to do. Susan dialed and ordered three pizza pies, going a little overboard and adding some breadsticks and melted cheese to the list. The driver recognized her address as the Sheridan place and said he would bring it as soon as possible. "My dad told me what's going on over there. All you girls back with your dad. You guys don't deserve to wait around for your pizza."

The Sheridan sisters and their father sat on the picnic table as another classic Vineyard sunsets drew itself over the horizon line and blurred the air with pinks and purple. Christine made sure everyone had a glass of wine, such was her way, and then sat and leaned against her hand and drew her eyes from their dad to Lola and back to Susan.

"When did you get in?" Wes finally asked his youngest, his hands flitting around on the top of the picnic table.

"Just this afternoon," Lola admitted. "It was surreal getting on the ferry again at Falmouth. It was as if no time had passed. I was still eighteen years old, getting off the island for the first time. On my own."

"I remember that day really well," Wes affirmed, his voice several notches lower than it had been. "I remember thinking that that was the last day I ever had to be a father."

"Had to be a father," Christine chimed in. "You make it sound like this horrible thing happened to you."

Wes's eyes looked troubled and far away for a moment. Susan swallowed, searching her mind for something to resolve the awkwardness. Finally, Wes gave a shrug. "I didn't mean it that way. I'm sorry."

There was a strange pause. Finally, Susan uttered, "It's okay, Dad. Really."

There was a knock at the door. Christine ambled up to go fetch the pizzas. Susan breathed a sigh of relief. They fell into easy conversation about pizzas: the toppings they liked, the places they frequented in their various cities. Lola insisted that the best pizza in the world came from Boston, and Christine scoffed at her. "Really? Because I think New Yorkers would fight you on that one. And they wouldn't be very nice about it!"

"You're all so worldly," Wes said, his smile wide and his lips heavy with grease. "I can't imagine the lives you've all had. All the experiences you've had. Susan, a criminal lawyer! You must have interacted with some of the strangest people. And Christine, working in all those restaurants! Lola, you must tell us—who have you interviewed with recently?"

Lola glowed with excitement. "I just had a big interview with an up-and-coming musician out of Boston. Very handsome. I think he will be famous, although it's always difficult to tell."

"And Lola. Your daughter. She must be what, ten now?" Wes said, scratching his head.

Lola's eyes darkened. Again, Susan felt the air shift. She sipped her wine a bit too quickly, waiting. This was Lola's fight to wage.

"Actually, Audrey is nineteen now," Lola said.

"Audrey is nineteen? You have got to be kidding me," he said.

"Nope. She's off at Penn State studying journalism."

"That must have been tough. Your first year with no kid at home, huh?" Susan said. "I remember when Amanda went away. I looked around our big house and wondered what it was all for."

"Luckily for me, I guess, I never had such a big place. It was just me and Audrey for so long," Lola said.

Again, Wes looked confused. He clucked his tongue and then pressed a napkin against his lips.

"Do you have something to say, Dad?" Lola asked.

"I just. That man. Audrey's father."

"Yeah?" Lola said.

Wes shifted. "Where did he go? I mean, did you... did you split up?"

Lola's face grew tense. Obviously, they'd gotten to the core of her issues much too quickly. Christine matched Susan with her wine drinking.

"That is just like you, Dad," Lola blurted.

Wes furrowed his brow. Obviously, he was confused and tilted his head to the side. "I'm sorry. Have I said something wrong again?"

"You just want to point out to me that I don't have the perfect little family you had. Isn't that right?" Lola blurted out as she held his stare.

She shot up from the picnic table and wound her hair into a ponytail. She looked frantic. "Timothy and I broke up fifteen years ago. I called you and told you when it happened. And don't you remember what you told me?"

Wes shook his head. He looked like a child who'd just gotten into a great deal of trouble at school.

"I told you that he was abusive. I told you that I

133

couldn't stay with him, no matter how hard I tried. And you told me that I should really work for it. You told me marriage takes work. You told me I needed to think of Audrey before I kicked him out," Lola sputtered. She looked on the verge of tears.

Wes dropped his chin to his chest and closed his eyes.

"He doesn't remember, Lola. Can you just please sit back down?" Susan murmured. She pressed her palm on Lola's arm to try and calm her, but it was no use.

"No. I can't just sit down, Susan," Lola said. Shooting up, she barreled down the porch steps and ambled toward the Sound. All three members of the Sheridan family looked at her as she raced across the rocks.

"Shoot," Christine murmured. She, too, shot up and raced toward Lola.

Susan remained at the table, unsure of what to do. She felt she couldn't leave her dad, not like this. The pain of the past twenty-five years lurked in a cloud over the top of all of them.

"Dad. Are you okay?" she finally asked. She looked at him to see—not the man Lola and Christine thought he was, but an older man with regrets.

"Yes. I'm okay," Wes said sadly. "I might head up to bed if that's okay."

"Of course. I know you must be tired after your long day."

Wes disappeared. Susan watched him creep up the steps. When the light turned out, she moved toward the porch steps and walked slowly toward her sisters. Lola stood near the water, her arms flailing as she had some kind of tantrum in conversation with Christine. When Susan reached them, Lola whirled around, her eyes bloodshot.

"Why did you bring us here, Susan?" Lola demanded. She smashed her palms on her thighs and balked. "You must think we're all just so willing to forgive and forget, like you, but we're not."

Susan collapsed on the rock next to Christine. Suddenly overwhelmed with everything, she burst into tears herself. Since she was the older sister, the one meant to keep it all together, both Christine and Lola huddled around her and held her close.

"I'm sorry. I'm sorry," Lola murmured into her ear. "I really didn't mean to be so harsh."

"No. I understand why you are. It's weird being here. I can feel her in everything. And Lola, you look..." Susan began.

"I know. I look just like her. It's horrible."

"And wonderful at the same time," Christine said. "It's like I'm seeing her again after so long. I only have a few photographs. I curse myself every single day because I don't have any more photographs."

The girls held one another there on the rocks for a long time, watching as the waves crashed into the shore. Susan heaved a sigh.

"Family drama, huh?" Christine said with a laugh. "I think that's our forte."

"I don't know anyone with more," Lola said, wiping a tear from her cheek.

"Susan, maybe it's about time you pulled out that weed pen," Christine said.

"What?" Lola asked, incredulous.

Susan shook her head. "No. I don't. I mean." She fumbled over her words. It couldn't be now.

After another moment of silence, Lola said, "I still think about that night all the time. When Dad came home drenched to his bones, he was screaming and crying at all of us to get out of the way, and then he just collapsed in a heap on the porch. Right where the picnic table is."

"I remember," Susan whispered.

"Susie, you tried to calm him down. You were only seventeen, and you acted like you were so much older. Ordering us to brew coffee and call Aunt Kerry. When Aunt Kerry got there, she had also been crying! That's when we knew something was really off," Christine said.

"A stupid boat accident," Lola mumbled.

"How could he have been so careless? He was always so safe on the water," Christine said. She said it like a plea, as though she needed to know why this reality was still their reality. "And the lights were off?"

"He would never talk about it," Susan said as she rubbed her hands together.

It was just what they'd heard from other people on the island. A tourist family had rammed themselves into their mother and father in the Nantucket Sound just after sunset. Their mother had drowned.

"They tell you about the finality of death, but they don't tell you that you have to keep going afterward," Lola murmured. "Now that I'm thirty-eight, I think about it all the time. I want to make sure Audrey still has me. I look three or four times before I cross the street. I hardly drink."

"You had to live here with him for years and years after it happened," Susan said suddenly. She pressed her lips together. "I should have done something about that."

"You were raising kids of your own," Lola said. "And you wanted to go to law school. You wanted to create a whole different world."

"We were all each other's baggage," Christine stated to her sisters.

It was harsh, but it reeked of truth. Susan shuddered and held her sisters closer to her. They wept over the next hour: for the mother they had lost, the father they weren't sure they could ever forgive, and all the time they'd lost with one another. It hadn't been their fault, but they hadn't handled it the way any of them might have wanted. This was the nature of gut-wrenching events in your life, Susan supposed. They happened like a bomb, and the debris was cast into all other areas of your existence. You thought you'd escaped it until you stood up and found another shard of glass in your leg.

"I thought maybe I wanted to leave," Lola said finally, sniffling. "But if Dad is as confused as you say, I can't really be so harsh with him."

"He's struggling for sure, and it's only going to get worse," Susan admitted. "And I could really use your help cleaning up the house and the inn if you're willing to help out."

"I don't have another assignment for a few weeks," Lola said. "And Audrey is away at an internship in Chicago. Like you, I guess, I don't have anything else to return to—for now. Plus, I can work remotely."

Slowly, the three sisters returned to their house. Like in the old days, Susan slept in her bedroom, while Lola and Christine shared the other, with its two twin beds. Susan closed her eyes and tried to imagine herself back in that summer before her mother had died.

The days they'd gone swimming and boating as a family.

The long sun-drenched day when they had shared a strawberry shortcake at Felix Neck.

The laughter, the love, the endless mother kisses.

Then, there was the screaming, the yelling, the seemingly endless abuse from their father. She and her sisters had listened to him tear at their mother throughout many nights as they'd quivered in their beds, wondering what would happen next.

Divorce had never been a possibility, not in their minds. It was the nineties, sure—a very pro-divorce era—but nobody in their family had divorced; neither had their friends.

And then, the accident happened.

The screaming hadn't stopped, though. It had barreled at them, the Sheridan sisters—a dirty secret they couldn't share with the rest of the island.

They had run. They had run as fast as they could away from this place.

And now, they were back.

And maybe it had all been a mistake.

Chapter Eighteen

The next day, Wes headed up to the Sunrise Cove Inn early, before any of the girls woke and joined him in the kitchen. This put a pit in Susan's stomach. Finally, she'd yanked her sisters all the way to this place, and already, enough of a storm had brewed to keep them all apart.

But Susan wasn't the kind of person to wallow. She was an action-oriented person who felt the steady dribble of wasted time and dreaded it. She brewed a pot of coffee, put on a pair of cut-off shorts and a tank top, and set to work on the kitchen itself. It needed deep-cleaning worse than any kitchen she had ever seen. One-by-one, Christine and Lola emerged from upstairs. Neither of them looked like their glittering city-selves in the morning. Both had bags under their eyes; both wore ratty t-shirts that Susan suspected they'd taken from men. Christine poured herself a cup of coffee and watched Susan without speaking for a moment.

"Is today the day you want to start in the house, then?"

Susan stopped her scrubbing and flared her nostrils. "What gave you that idea?"

"Lola! Guess what? Susan's got her sarcasm turned up to eleven."

"Fantastic," Lola called in from the porch, where she performed another yoga stretch.

After a bit of grumbling, Christine led the sisters through the living area, the small parlor that seemed completely untouched since they'd left, and then up into their father's bedroom, where they were shocked to find their mother's clothes still hanging as though she was about to return to the house and change.

Lola whistled. "I can't believe he's just gotten up every single morning, opened the closet, and looked at these clothes. I think I would have had a nervous breakdown."

On the far end of the rack hung one of their mother's favorite lilac dresses, with light lace detail on the top and a skirt that swung out wide when their father twirled her. Christine pulled it out a bit more to get a full view of it. In her mind, her mother twirled out and then twirled back into her father, midway through whatever festival dance, seemingly countless.

"Wow, that dress. I can't believe how dated it looks," Christine marveled. "In my memory, it was the most beautiful thing I'd ever seen."

"Let me have it," Lola said with her hands outstretched. She swung it off the hanger, then swiftly removed her shorts and t-shirt and pulled the lilac dress on. It fit her like a glove. Although her makeup hadn't been done and her hair was pulled up, she looked glamorous, as if she had stepped out of a magazine from another time.

And again, she looked even more like their mother.

Christine and Susan followed Lola's lead, taking their favorite garments from their racks and zipping, buttoning, twirling, and laughing. Christine snapped on the old radio on the bedside table and played tunes from the long-lost nineties summers.

"Let's get rid of most of it," Susan said. "But keep our favorite dresses. Dad wouldn't want all of it to go."

They made piles of things: the clothes they didn't remember that could easily be dropped off at a second-hand store, the ratty ones that clearly didn't belong anywhere except a landfill, and ones that seemed unclear to them and required a conversation with their father. The work went easily and united them. They didn't talk of anything serious, not of the accident or their father, or even their messed-up lives back in Boston, Newark, and New York.

Afterward, Christine stepped down the hall and peered up at the attic door. "I bet we can put any leftover stuff in the attic to give Dad some more room."

"Not a bad idea," Susan affirmed. "I don't even know if I've ever been up there."

Lola, who'd changed out of the lilac dress by then, burst forward, grabbed the little string, and yanked the attic door down with a flourish. A ladder swung down, nearly whacking them all in the head.

"Hey!" Christine cried.

"Sorry," Lola said with a laugh.

This was just like Lola. Never thinking before acting. But already, Lola surged up the ladder and entered the dusty attic. "Wow!" she exclaimed. "Hate to break it to you girls, but it looks like there's more stuff of Mom's up here."

Christine grumbled, but Susan sneaked up the ladder almost immediately. She had grown addicted to these memories of her mother. She wanted to touch more objects, to try on more clothes, and feel what her mother might have felt.

Sure enough, it seemed their father had put even more clothes up there, along with several boxes of books and several old high school yearbooks. They'd been high school sweethearts and were featured in the front of the senior issue as "Cutest Couple," where they found both of their photos since they'd been high school sweethearts.

"Can you believe how young she looks?" Christine muttered, flashing the yearbook around for the other two to see.

"She looks just like Amanda," Susan said.

"How old is Amanda again?" Lola asked.

"Twenty-two. I can hardly believe it myself."

"We really have to get her and Audrey together," Lola said.

Susan's heart felt squeezed. "Yes. I think that's a fantastic idea. Both of them are career girls, though. My Amanda just started her own internship at a law firm."

"Ha! And mine will be a journalist. They take after their old mothers," Lola said, letting out a small laugh.

Christine remained quiet. She stepped toward what looked like a dusty old chest in the corner and bent in front of it. "This looks really old. I don't remember it at all. Do either of you?"

Susan reflected. "I remember Mom's dad giving over a lot of antiques at one point. Maybe this is one of them?"

"Maybe," Christine said. She reached for the lock that hung off it and yanked at it. It wasn't locked and whipped apart. She then removed it and slowly opened the chest.

Inside was even more of their mother's memorabilia. In fact, it seemed as if their father had made this a shrine to her life. At the top were several photographs of their mother in various stages of motherhood. There, she held Susan and only Susan, her only baby at the time, while seated on a dock with her feet hanging in the water.

"Look at that hair!" Lola whispered. She lifted the photo and gazed at it with enormous eyes.

There were many more photos, with complete photo albums from various stages of their young lives and several pictures of their father and mother together. Their wedding photo remained in a frame, their father broad-shouldered and handsome, beaming down at his young and beautiful bride.

"I wanted Mom at my wedding so bad," Susan mumbled. "When I was a bridesmaid for other girlfriends, I would watch them with their mothers. They always said the sweetest things right before walking down the aisle. It always seemed so big and so important."

Christine delicately removed things from the chest and lined them up on the floor. These were obviously things they would keep, back up digitally, and maybe even divide among them.

"Whoa," Christine said again. Her eyes were locked on something else in the chest. "There are some diaries down here."

Lola gasped. "I didn't know Mom wrote in a diary!"

"She always did," Susan insisted, knowing that maybe at age twelve, that hadn't been the kind of thing Lola was looking out for.

Christine removed the diaries and placed them next to the other photographs. Then, she stopped dead as she peered deeper into the chest. Her face looked stricken. It was as if she had really seen a ghost.

"Christine. You look scared. What's up?" Lola asked as she chewed her bottom lips in anticipation.

Christine reached into the chest with shaking hands and drew out three sealed envelopes. On each of the envelopes, their mother had written out their names in perfect penmanship:

Susan

Christine

Lorraine

The three girls stared down at the weather letters. It seemed as if their mother had just sent them. As if she knew they were all together for the first time and had chosen this moment to pass them along.

"How... how did she write these and leave them for us?" Lola blurted. "What are they?"

Susan shook her head. Her heart sank into her stomach. "I have no idea."

"What did she want to write a letter to us about?" Christine demanded. "Did she have secrets or something?"

Susan considered her own affinity for secrets: all that she hid from her sisters, all that she hid from her children. All that she hid from herself.

But Lola erupted with anger and passion and fear. She looked on the verge of toppling over. "No. I cannot handle this right now," she cried. Tears swelled in her eyes.

"I just. I don't understand," Christine whispered.

Lola fled. She nearly fell down the ladder but gripped the rungs at the last minute and landed on the hallway floor safely. Christine hustled toward the ladder too. It seemed as if they ran from ghosts. Susan sighed and collected the photographs and other memorabilia and returned them to the chest. She placed the diaries and the letters on top.

"What did you want to tell us?" she said quietly.

Downstairs, she found Christine and Lola on the porch with a bottle of wine opened. It was only noon, but it felt as though they'd time-traveled from a great distance. Susan collapsed on the porch swing next to them and accepted her own glass. The three of them didn't find words for a long time.

"It's like she knew," Lola murmured. "She knew we would be here today. She knew that we needed some way to come together."

"That's ridiculous. Mom has been dead for twenty-five years," Christine returned.

"I just felt like she was always honest with us," Lola said. "Unlike Dad."

"But how much could we have possibly known about Mom?" Susan said suddenly.

Both Christine and Lola gave her perturbed looks. "What do you mean?" Lola demanded.

"Just think about all the secrets you have kept from Audrey over the years," she said, looking directly at Lola. "Think about everything you had to keep to yourself if only to keep her safe or keep a little piece of yourself for only yourself."

Lola shook her head vehemently. "I tell Audrey everything."

Susan had a feeling that wasn't truthful, but she couldn't insist on it. They sipped their wine and gazed out at the water, each stirring in their own panicked thoughts. Obviously, whatever lurked in those letters had the capacity to change their lives forever. And maybe they weren't ready for that just yet.

Chapter Nineteen

Things settled into an even pattern after that. Christine, Susan, and Lola shared house responsibilities, deep-cleaning, scrubbing, taking trips to the secondhand store, and making nightly dinners for the remainder of the Sheridan clan. Sometimes, they had everyone from the family over—Aunt Kerry, Uncle Trevor, cousins, and whoever else was around. It was mid-June and inching toward late June, and Susan felt time dribbling between her fingers. Days with Wes Sheridan were always a toss-up. Sometimes, he seemed sharp as an arrow, vibrant and ready to make jokes and banter with the best of them. Other days, he seemed hazy-eyed and overly willing to stay in bed for many hours at a time. These days, Susan took over the brunt of the work at the inn.

Susan now had a good grip on the day-to-day events at the Sunrise Cove Inn. As the weeks passed, she felt closer and closer with her mother, who had spent most of her final years at the Sunrise Cove, giving her life to the demanding pleasure of hospitality. Susan was genuinely surprised at how good she was at this. After years as a criminal lawyer, she was glad to say cheerful hellos, shake hands, and grow close to families over their visits, only to feel really sad when they returned home. When she told Amanda this over the phone, she said, "Who are you, and what have you done with my mother?"

Still, it bothered Susan that she hadn't been able to figure out where a lot of the money was going. It seemed they had to constantly order new food and supplies, and the accounts were bled out quicker and quicker. She resolved to get to the bottom of it, but there were also about eight zillion other things to "get to the bottom" of at the moment. Patience, she would tell herself. She had to be patient.

Dinners between the four remaining Sheridans weren't always easy, but nothing ever grew as tense as it had on that first night of Lola's arrival. Lola very quickly recognized Wes's dementia and tried her best to remain upbeat. Susan also suspected that the letters had added a jolt of confusion to the situation. The world didn't seem entirely black or white anymore, although they weren't overly willing to forgive their father for anything any time soon.

June 20 was the yearly Oak Bluffs Harbor Festival. Both Lola and Christine resolved to stay through it, although Susan could sense they had begun to grow restless. The days were summery and beautiful; the water was constantly pristine. Scott had even taken the three of them out on his boat a few times. They'd donned their swimsuits, leaped into the waves, and hollered at the big, impossibly blue sky, and Scott had laughed and stayed on the boat with a beer in hand. "The three of you haven't changed at all since you were teenagers.

Did anyone ever give you a sign that it was time to grow up?"

"Never," Lola said with a wink.

On these boat trips, Susan always sat up front with Scott while he drove. She felt strangely pulled to him, although they'd done nothing but talk so far. When she glanced his way, she felt her heart surge with the memory of her love for him. But was that love something she wanted again? So much of her existence was tied up in dishonesty at the moment. Still, she could feel his love for her coming off him in waves. The attraction was most definitely still there.

On the morning of the Oak Bluffs Harbor Festival, Susan awoke with more pain than she had experienced in several months. She held the rail as she hobbled downstairs and sat at the edge of the porch with her legs swinging in the air in front of her. She sucked on her weed pen, closed her eyes, and willed herself to keep her cool throughout the day. She had looked forward to it for weeks since Amanda had said she would come to the island for the festival. She had only met Lola and Christine once each before, and neither time together. Lola had also decided to bring Audrey out to the Vineyard for a long weekend. "I said I would pay for the flights. I guess she can pay me back when she becomes a famous journalist," Lola had said.

Regardless, Susan wasn't willing to let a little pain get in her way.

Lola, Christine, and Susan drove to the ferry dock at ten in the morning. Miraculously, Audrey and Amanda had nabbed the same ferry that morning. According to several hilarious text messages, the girls had been able to find each other almost instantly.

> Amanda: I mean, we look alike, Mom.
> Like sisters, even though we are first
> cousins.

The girls sent a selfie from the deck of the ferry. Lola and Susan nearly lost their minds over it.

"They finally met each other!" Susan cried.

When the ferry arrived, it was obvious that Amanda and Audrey had spent the entire ride digging into the gritty details of each other's lives, asking questions, and swapping secrets. They walked down the ramp from the ferry in the middle of raucous laughter. When Amanda lifted her eyes to find her mother, she immediately bolted forward and wrapped her arms around her.

"Mom! Wow, you look fantastic," she said, breaking the hug and beaming at her. "Seriously. You're glowing."

"She's probably spent more time in the sun over the past few weeks than she has in years," Lola said. "It's so good to see you again, Amanda. You look beautiful. And that ring! Susan hasn't been able to shut up about your engagement."

Big hugs came next: Susan and Audrey, Christine and Amanda, Lola and Audrey, again and again, and again, with little kisses on her forehead and cries of, "My little Chicago journalist!"

Audrey was the spitting image of Lola. Her mannerisms were the same along with her chestnut hair; they dressed the same, and they seemed on the verge of flying off the wall at any moment with their bright eyes. Amanda was much more level-headed, like Susan, she supposed, and looked at Audrey and Lola as if they were co-conspirators, on the verge of taking over the world.

The sisters piled the suitcases into the back of the car

and then drove back to the main house. Susan tried to point out as much as she could to the girls—the Sunrise Cove Inn, which already looked much better than it had weeks before, and the little hiking trails, coves, and old friends' houses. Both Amanda and Audrey seemed in awe of the place.

"You can't be serious. You grew up here?" Amanda said as she cut out from the car at the main house and peered down the hill at the Sound below. "I can't believe it. It's so beautiful here."

Susan tried to see the place through Amanda's eyes. It was probably a quarter of the size of the place she had grown up within Newark, with its own set of crooked shutters and chipped paint. But it also beamed with charm and goodwill. Amanda and Audrey grabbed their bags and hopped up into the house. It had been agreed that the girls would sleep on the pullout couch down-stairs. They immediately changed into their swimsuits and rushed toward the water below to leap in.

"Look at them," Christine said, looking out the window. "They're so young! Their whole lives ahead of them."

"I wonder if Amanda will want to have her wedding on the island," Lola said. "Charlotte and Rachel have really picked up business with their event coordinating. Oh my gosh! And Claire does flowers..."

"It's almost like they were all lying in wait for us, just to give Amanda and Chris the perfect wedding." Susan laughed.

Late that afternoon, Christine, Susan, Lola, Amanda, and Audrey donned summer dresses and headed to the Oak Bluffs Harbor Festival. The festival simmered with electricity and life. A live band played old hits from a podium while people danced below. A large Ferris wheel inched around and around, showing its riders an immaculate view of Oak Bluffs and the surrounding areas. Susan remembered one of the first harbor festivals with Scott. They'd ridden the Ferris wheel and kissed at the top, her heart performing a little tap dance across her stomach.

At the festival, the girls ate, laughed, and walked around, greeting several other Vineyard locals and introducing them to Amanda and Audrey. To most everyone, it was obvious that Audrey and Amanda were "Sheridan girls."

Amanda fell into step with Susan and slipped her fingers through her hand as she had done when she had been much younger. "You didn't tell me that everyone on Martha's Vineyard knew your name," she said with a sly smile.

"Ha. It's a tiny place. Everyone knows each other and everyone else's business. Now that they know you, I'm sure they're gossiping about you too," Susan said.

"I love it. We didn't have that kind of thing in Newark growing up," Amanda replied.

Susan's stomach dropped like a stone. "Would you have preferred living here?"

Amanda shrugged. "I just think it's interesting that it wasn't an option. That's all."

Susan nodded contemplatively. "I have considered staying. At least till the end of this summer season. Then, who knows?"

"You're working really hard. Christine said that you've been at the inn almost every day since you got here," Amanda said. Her brow furrowed with worry.

"Yes, but you know me. I like hard work."

"You're crazy," Amanda said. "But I get it. It's good to

throw yourself into something after everything that's happened. I think Jacob and Kristen are a bit perturbed that they don't have that live-in babysitter they were promised."

Susan laughed good-naturedly. "Can you imagine me living as a live-in babysitter? As much as I love those babies, I don't think I could hack it. Not for very long, anyway."

"Audrey says she hardly knows her dad," Amanda continued. "That he ran off when she was little. I think his name is Timothy?"

Susan nodded. "None of us knew him. One day, Lola had a boyfriend. The next, she had a baby. And then the next, many, many years went by—and now, we're here, trying to make up for lost time."

That night, everyone gathered at the main house for a barbecue and to watch the fireworks blare out across the water. Aunt Kerry, Uncle Trevor, all their children, and many of their grandchildren and great-grandchildren ambled in with a wide variety of delicious snacks, main course meals, desserts, and crates of beer and bottles of wine. There was always more than enough to go around, but this took the cake.

Wes arrived from the Sunrise Cove Inn just after six thirty. He scrubbed his forehead of summertime sweat and beamed at Audrey and Amanda with confused yet happy eyes. Susan assumed that he thought he had looked at his wife or his daughters again.

But Wes surprised her. "These must be my beautiful granddaughters," he beamed at them.

Aunt Kerry gave Susan a knowing look. Maybe he wasn't as far gone as they'd all assumed. Maybe there was still time.

"Hey, Grandpa," Audrey said. "You have a really beautiful place here."

"I can't believe you get to see the water every day," Amanda said.

"It's a little slice of heaven. That's what your grandmother always used to say," Wes said. He hugged them close. "Now, Amanda, Susie told me that you're engaged to be married." He released them and smiled wider. "Tell me. Is the guy good enough for you?"

Amanda chuckled and blushed. She'd missed out on this kind of conversation her entire life. Susan's gaze traced across the room as Amanda answered good-naturedly. Suddenly, there was a holler from the back door. Scott Frampton appeared with another crate of beer and a big bag of ice, which they'd tended to need as of late for these bigger parties. Susan felt her face nearly stretch in half with her grin. Scott bent and gave her a small kiss on the cheek—just a greeting, nothing more. Still, the contact was almost more than Susan could bear.

"There he is. Our ice savior," Lola said. She yanked one of the big coolers out from the kitchen closet and immediately filled it with ice.

"Mom!" Audrey said with a laugh as Lola began to sling beers into the ice like some kind of Vineyard barbecue expert. She made eye contact with Susan and said, "I've never seen her look so..."

"Domestic?" Lola said as she snapped up and swiped her icy hands across her lap.

"I guess that's the word," Audrey said.

"What can I say? I'm my mother's daughter," Lola said.

Later that night, as the sun inched lower beneath the horizon line, Lola, Christine, Susan, Amanda, and

Audrey sat out on the porch in a haze of wine and conversation. Christine peppered Amanda with questions about her wedding, leaning toward her "chipper-drunk" personality, which Susan was grateful about.

"You have to let me make your cake," Christine insisted.

"She's a pastry chef," Susan explained. "One of the best in New York."

"I don't know about that. But I do know my way around a cake," Christine said with a laugh.

"I just think it's fantastic. You have your career, your fiancé, and your entire life before you," Lola said. "And you're close with your brother, it sounds like?"

Amanda nodded and blushed. She seemed to sense how awkward this question was. After all, the Sheridan sisters had gone so many years without many conversations at all.

"Good. Hold on to him," Lola said. Her voice was heavy, intense. "He's much more important than you can fully realize right now. You can't imagine what it feels like to have lost so much time."

There, at the picnic table, the three Sheridan sisters and the next generation of Sheridan women placed their hands in the center of the table, a kind of allegiance to the love of their family and how they needed to rebuild it, make it stronger and better than ever so that it would never tear apart again.

Chapter Twenty

Several days later, Amanda and Audrey left the island. Christine and Lola headed off for a boat ride with one of Lola's old school friends, while Susan headed back to the Sunrise Cove Inn. Natalie had a few doctors appointments that day, and she wanted to check on some of the details Scott had fixed up while she had taken days off to spend time with her daughter.

When she reached the front desk, she found a little letter on the counter with her name on it. It jolted her with the memory of the letters that waited for them in the attic. Still, the handwriting was none other than Scott's. She would have recognized it anywhere, from long-lost notes he had written her when they'd first dated in high school.

Susie,

Thanks again for the invitation to be with your family the other day. Your daughter is incredibly intelligent and kind and inquisitive. It was a pleasure to speak with her for a while about her life as a soon-to-be big-shot criminal lawyer (like her beautiful mom).

I wanted to let you know that I have to run out for a few freight responsibilities, but I stopped into the Inn this morning to finish up painting the back side near the office window. The Inn is almost back to her old glory. Let's keep working on it! We're so close!

Yours,

Scott

Susan heaved a sigh and pressed the letter against her chest. With her eyes closed and her mind racing, she hardly heard the dark and gritty voice from the doorway leading to the bistro.

"Susan? Are you all right?"

Susan opened her eyes to find Chuck smirking at her. He clearly didn't care about her well-being and only wanted to point out her daydream. She dropped the letter from her chest and quickly folded it up as Chuck approached. When he reached the front desk, he blinked down to see the envelope with her name on it in Scott's clear handwriting.

"I see my brother is in the habit of writing you love letters again," Chuck said.

Susan kept a false smile across her lips. "No love letters here. Can I do anything for you, Chuck? Everything okay in the delivery?"

Chuck clucked his tongue. "Better than ever, Susie. Better than ever. The inn certainly looks good. The paint job? The new shutters?"

"All thanks to your brother," Susan said. "I don't know what we would have done without him."

Chuck's eyebrows rose. He chuckled strangely. "I guess he probably did all that for free?"

"Yes, he did. It was really kind of him."

Chuck splayed both his hands across the front desk.

His fingernails were filled with grime and dirt. "I guess you probably couldn't have afforded anyone these days to fix it up. It would have really set you back, huh?"

Susan studied the strange sneer he wore across his weathered face. His dark eyes sent a shiver through her body. There was something really off about it. She was reminded of a previous client she'd had six or seven years ago. He had robbed a local store—but that hadn't been the worst of his crimes. The worst was that he'd lied and schemed and manipulated his girlfriend into going along with it. He had looked and spoken to both Susan and his girlfriend in exactly the way Chuck did just now.

He spoke as if he knew he was getting away with something. He spoke as if he took pleasure in it.

"I mean, what with all the setbacks the inn has had over the past few years," Chuck added.

It was the final sword in the belly. Susan stretched her smile wider. "To be honest, I think we'll probably be okay."

"I hope so. The Sunrise Cove Inn is an institution around here. When we were kids, I remember hanging out near this very inn and seeing you, your sisters, and your mom and dad out near the water. Just over there." Chuck nodded toward the window, and Susan couldn't resist flashing her head around and blinking down at the strange memory, now transcribed from Chuck's own mind.

"We would do anything for the inn," Susan said. "It was our mother and father's greatest treasure."

"It's too bad about old Wes, huh?" Chuck said. He seemed willing to say anything to goad her. "He was always such a sharp guy. Really makes you think about aging, doesn't it?"

Susan had never smacked anyone in her life, but she really, really wanted to do it now. After a strange pause, she said, "Anyway, is there anything I can do for you, Chuck? I would love to help you out if I can."

"Nope! Just wanted to stop in and say hi. See you around." He tipped his baseball hat and then sauntered back down the hallway toward the bistro, which led out to the parking lot on the other side.

Susan furrowed her brow and turned toward the current month's accounting ledger. The back of her head felt all dizzy and strange as it had in previous lawyer days when her mind started.

It didn't take long for Susan to notice a pattern.

She couldn't believe she hadn't seen it before.

On the days that she didn't operate at the inn —the days when either her father or Natalie manned the front desk—someone else's handwriting listed the orders and the amounts paid for the supplies delivered from Frampton Freights. Each slot corresponded with a receipt, which was stored in the back of the book. Each receipt held Chuck's and Scott's signature on it, along with Wes's or Natalie's, along with a list of all the items that had been delivered to the inn and bistro that day.

Flour. Sugar. Tomatoes, both cherry and Roma. Cucumbers, green peppers, onions, olives. Several different types of fruits, including blueberries, blackberries, and raspberries. There were fresh towels, sheets, tons of laundry detergent, and other various items, depending on what Wes and Natalie (and, now, Susan) decided to order for the inn. They had anywhere between twenty-five and thirty guests per day staying at the Sunrise Cove Inn, and they could host up to one hundred people per night in the bistro, sometimes more. The menu was constantly changing; people were always coming and going.

And somehow, some way, it seemed that Frampton Freight was overcharging them for nearly every single shipment.

And they didn't overcharge with a few pennies here and there.

No.

It seemed as if over the span of several months, they'd taken anywhere between one hundred to two-hundred and fifty dollars extra per delivery. This meant that in a period of only thirty days, they could take, at the minimum, three thousand dollars.

Throughout Susan's excavation, her heart pounded with anger and resentment, and fear. Was it possible that Scott had gotten closer to her over the past few weeks to ensure that his and Chuck's scheme could keep going? He flirted with her, buttered her up, and made her feel like a teenager again, all for their damn scam.

And it was certainly possible that Frampton Freight was doing this to other businesses in the Vineyard.

Susan felt delirious and sick to her stomach. She dropped back in the chair that always rested near the front desk and stared straight ahead. Tears itched to pour out of her eyes, but she forced them to stay in. The last thing she needed to do at the Sunrise Cove Inn was to make the guests think the front desk lady was a crazy person. She forced herself to smile and greet as many of the guests as she could over the next few hours until Natalie appeared to release her.

The second they were alone, Susan showed Natalie the receipts and how they didn't seem to line up with how frequently they had to order new supplies.

Susan turned to her then. "Based on everything that's on these receipts and in the ledgers, we've been over-ordering and spending way too much over the past eight months? Nine months? Maybe longer."

Natalie's eyes swam with panic. "Are you saying that Frampton Freight has been stealing from us? I didn't notice anything, Susan. How could I be so stupid? How could I...?"

"Don't think of it that way," Susan said. "It's not your fault."

Admittedly, Susan was a tiny, tiny bit annoyed at Natalie for not noticing this in the first place. After all, during this time, her father had been falling deeper into his dementia diagnosis, and the weight should have fallen on Natalie's shoulders. It was part of her job, after all.

On the other hand, it wasn't like people on the Vine-yard to steal from one another. Especially not people who had grown up there and known one another for decades.

"I have to run off and get to the bottom of this," Susan told Natalie. "I'm going to take one of the company cars."

Natalie bobbed her head, still lost in thought. "I still can't believe this. I can't imagine anyone doing this to us. In Oak Bluffs? We're all supposed to be family. We're supposed to support each other."

Susan paused and gave her a sad smile. She'd been off the island for long enough to know that that sort of bleary-eyed nostalgia didn't hold out. Even Scott, the man she had assumed loved her beyond anything else, loved her beyond the years that they'd missed with each other, had wronged her. She had to keep a tiny sliver of the cold heart of the criminal lawyer, the woman wronged by the secretary and her husband—the cliché, through and through.

Susan tore the car down the road that led to Scott's house, her lips muttering as she drove too fast. When she reached his place, the tires braked to a loud stop against the stones and kicked them back out. At the sound, Scott yanked open the back door and stepped out. Immediately, he grinned widely—his eyes reflecting what she had always assumed was his again-growing love for her.

She was a damn fool.

She busted out of the car and marched up to him. He quickly recognized that she wasn't there for some kind of flirtation. His smile fell, and he furrowed his brow.

"Susan, what's going on?" he asked, looking confused. She was reminded of their long-ago high school fights when she'd spontaneously broken up with him (and then immediately gotten back with him the next day—such was the life of a teenager).

When she reached him, she inhaled deeply. Unfortunately, a tear slid down her cheek and drew a thin line toward her chin. She had wanted to be strong while she told him she knew what he had done.

"Susan, you're scaring me," Scott whispered.

He reached out to grab her hand, but she yanked it back just as fast.

"Don't pretend you don't know," she said, her voice harsh.

"You're going to have to help me out here," Scott said. His eyes looked glossy and strange.

"Help you out? I mean, it really should have been obvious from the start why you were so willing to give up all your time to the inn. You felt guilty about the past eight-odd months you've been stealing from us. But Scott, how could you do it? You know that the inn is the most important thing in our family. My mother and father gave everything to that place. It's the only thing we have left. And you were willing to run it into the ground."

Scott furrowed his brow and studied her face for a long time.

"Don't just stand there. Don't make me feel like a bigger idiot than I already am," Susan said.

Suddenly, Scott whipped out his arms and grasped her elbows. His hands were powerful, and his grip was tight. He held her as he had when she had first lost her mother—as though they were out to sea and she was about to tip into the water if not for his sturdy frame.

"Susan Sheridan, I wouldn't lie to you. I never have, and I never will. I don't know anything about any money taken from the Sunrise Cove Inn. But if you say this is true, then it is. I know you wouldn't lie to me, either."

Susan swallowed. She felt a deep cavern between them. Was it possible that she was the one lacking the honesty between them?

"I checked and double-checked the ledgers and all the receipts. Everything," Susan finally said. Her voice shook. "It doesn't add up. And we're losing money all the time. I don't understand it."

Scott nodded. His voice was gruff, and his eyes burned with anger. "Susan, I promise you, I'll get to the bottom of this. Don't think about it any longer. Whatever has been taken from you won't be taken anymore. And if it all works out, I can get it all back."

"What are you going to do?" Susan asked as she stood there with her hands on her hips.

"I don't know," Scott returned. "But I told myself I would never let you down. Not again."

Chapter Twenty-One

S usan drove around after she left Scott's. She gripped the steering wheel a little too hard and played the radio a little too loud. Occasionally, she felt a scream erupt out from between her lips—all that pent-up anger and fear and sadness over the past few months accumulating in this enormous sound.

Did she believe Scott didn't know anything about the money? That it was all Chuck's doing? She didn't know. After so many years of marriage to Richard, she hadn't wanted to believe that he planned to leave her for a secretary, either. But he had. And maybe Scott had stolen from her father too. All those things could exist in the same realm.

This was the realm in which her father had been the one driving the boat at night without his lights on. The boat that had, at one moment, carried her mother, and the next, had tipped her into the dangerous waves.

Her death had cast ripples through their small family and their small community.

It had been foolish of her to come back to Martha's Vineyard.

Nothing lurked on the island but pain and misfortune.

Even her father was on his last legs—probably just a few years from devastation and death.

What then? Would she stay on the island as a divorcée? Manning the front desk at the inn?

What was left of her life but memories?

Just after dusk, Susan arrived back at the main house. When she entered, she found a half-eaten lasagna on the countertop and a nearly finished bottle of red wine next to it. Her sister's voices carried in from the porch. Slowly, she poured her own glass of wine and joined Christine and Lola, her heart thudding slowly. There, on the picnic table before the girls, were the three envelopes with the names LORRAINE, CHRISTINE, and SUSAN stitched across them in perfect penmanship. Beside them was the stack of old diaries.

Christine and Lola turned their heads quickly, their eyes glossy from wine.

"What's wrong with you?" Christine asked.

Susan let her shoulders sag forward. "It's a long story."

She joined them at the table and gazed down at the letters. It had been a while since they'd discovered them— time enough to sit with the fact that they existed. She felt overwhelmed by her altercation with Scott and her newfound understanding of the money taken and all the wild, frantic driving across the island. Even the smells in the house, the lilac bushes, the red wine, and the baked lasagna filled her with a sense of longing and sadness she could hardly understand.

"We figured it was time since Christine has to head back to the city in a few days," Lola said. "And it's no use hiding from something like this. Technically they've existed for over twenty-five years."

"It's time we know what she wanted to say," Christine said.

"Okay. I guess there's no time like the present," Susan whispered.

Each of the Sheridan sisters took their letter and held it up. They agreed to open them on the count of three.

"One." Christine breathed.

"Two," Lola said quietly.

"Three," Susan finished.

With that, they tore open the old envelopes and brought out yellowed stationery with their mother's perfect handwriting rippled across in neat lines. All three studied theirs for a long time without making a single sound.

Beautiful Susie,

You're seventeen years old. Seventeen years old and with far more responsibility on your shoulders than most girls your age should have to deal with. I can see it already in your face and your mannerisms: you're only a few seconds from being a full-fledged woman with her own husband and children and responsibilities. And I know you'll take it all on with finesse and intelligence.

You're reading this today because I've left your father to take a little time to think.

Please don't panic. I'm still on the island, not far, and I will come if you really, really need me. But for now, I'm asking you for a bit of space and a bit of time.

Since your father and I took over the Sunrise Cove Inn

and had you three girls, we've devoted nearly every minute of our time and effort to you, Christine, Lola, and our numerous guests. Perhaps you've noticed how difficult it has been for your father and me over the years. We don't get along like we used to. We scream and bicker and fight—and it shames me to know that you've heard us, night after night. It isn't how I would have written the story of my family life.

I've fallen in love with someone else. It's complicated, and I don't always know if it's the sort of love I want to keep with me forever—but it's very real, and it's at the forefront of my mind at the moment. I would be doing myself a tremendous disservice if I didn't follow through with it and see it from all sides.

This does not mean that I love you any less. On the contrary, I hope this rather "selfish" step that I'm taking will force you, always, to double-check every inch of your life. Is your partner making you happy? Have you made the right choice in your career? Are you ensuring every single portion of your life thrills you, excites you, and makes you want to get up in the morning?

I love you, Susie. You were my first baby and my first real love. Remember that I'll always be here for you to lend an ear. Thank you for reading.

Love, Mom

Tears formed rivers down her cheeks and down her chin. She turned her head to find Christine and Lola both in similar states. Their shoulders all slumped forward as they sat in silence and listened to the waves shudder up on the shore.

Christine stood, disappeared for a moment, and returned with a full bottle of red. With a flourish, she cranked the top off and poured the three of them another sturdy glass. They sipped and cried and sipped and cried, all without making a single sound.

Their mother had planned to leave their father.

"Who was it?" Lola finally said, looking at both her sisters through blurry eyes.

It was the only question they could really ask. Christine closed her eyes, then clenched them as she drank down half of her glass.

"I can't remember her talking to anyone except her friends and our family and Dad," Christine said after she finished. "She was always smiling and laughing with everyone. It really could be anyone."

Susan's eyes turned toward the diaries. Without a word, she lifted the first and studied the inner page, which read 1987-1988. "She died in 1993," she whispered. "Which means any diary from around then would tell us."

Lola and Christine exchanged glances as though this stepped too far over the line. Maybe they didn't actually want to know.

"We've come this far. I think we should just go for it," Susan murmured.

The fourth diary she lifted started in the year 1992, late season. She turned a few pages to find the first mention of this stranger and started to read aloud.

August 24, 1992

I can't get him out of my mind. He stops by the Inn when he knows Wes isn't around, last time with lilacs. He knows they're my favorite. We sneak out behind the Inn at dusk, and he whispers in my ear that he'll take me away from here—he has that fabulous boat—and we'll run as fast as we can away from the Vineyard, away from anyone who knows our name.

Sometimes, I wonder if I rushed into all of it: the marriage to Wes, the three girls. I couldn't have known it at the time. I was just a baby, just a girl.

The diary continued with various entries about this mystery man, along with random mentions of Lola, Christine, and Susan. "Christine is so surly sometimes. I don't know what's gotten into her. She broke up with yet another boyfriend. It's really like she doesn't want to be happy."

At this, Christine said, "Not a lot has changed, I guess." Her cheeks burned red with sadness.

September 5, 1992

Slowly but surely, the tourists are leaving for the year. I'm glad to see them go, but Wes is angry. He thinks we didn't make enough money this year, and I can see it on his face; he blames me.

The girls just started school again. Susan is almost seventeen and in her junior year of high school. Christine is almost fourteen, and my darling Lola will be twelve soon. I love them to pieces, but now, even Lola has something of a life of her own. Friends, boyfriends, events; they all want time away from Wes and me. Certainly, the fighting between us has been reason enough to stay away.

But this means I've been able to steal more time with Stan. We like to make love on his boat at night with the beautiful moon hanging in the air above us. It's a feeling I've never had before.

With that, Susan whipped her head up, her eyes enormous. "Stan. Stan Ellis," she whispered.

Christine's and Lola's jaws dropped. "The fisherman?" they asked in unison.

"That's the only Stan I know," Susan said quietly, her mind racing.

"Did Mom really have an affair with that old fisherman we always see out there on the Sound?" Lola asked in complete shock. She pressed her hand across her forehead, seeming to feel the full weight of this new information.

"And it sounds like Dad knew all about it," Susan said, scanning another entry. "Listen to this."

September 22, 1992

Wes and I got into another familiar fight. He insists that we can find our way out of this. That we can be the old lovers we used to be. But I have no idea how to find love for him again. All he says is how much he loves me and how he wants to fix this. But in my mind—fixing it means tearing it apart. I want to leave him so desperately, which makes him cling to the Inn and to me and to the girls all the more. He yells and screams all through the night. Sometimes, he cries. I can hardly take it.

"Oh my god," Lola murmured, placing a hand over her mouth.

"Dad loved her so much," Christine said, her eyes wide. "And then... he took her out on the boat and—"

"But don't you think it's possible that it wasn't Mom and Dad on the boat that night?" Susan asked suddenly. She felt the question ticking across her brain, stepping lightly like a spider.

Lola furrowed her brow. "What do you mean?"

"Like, we know Stan had a boat. That they liked to go out on it," Susan said.

"And do a lot more than that," Christine said.

"Yes. But do you remember anything else about the accident? Do you remember anything about the newspaper report? Other people were in the accident. Remember? The lights were off, and two other people died," Susan said, trying to recall everything.

Christine and Lola looked lost. In the haze of their collective grief, all the girls had avoided news reports as much as they could and kept to themselves. Susan, in particular, had latched herself to Scott without letting go until, of course, she'd abandoned him for a better life after graduation.

"Two other people died?" Lola demanded. She grabbed her phone and entered the date: "June 3, 1993," along with "Martha's Vineyard boating accident."

Her mouth formed into a round O. "Yes. Two tourists named Monica Zehlendorf and her boyfriend, Marcus Thompkins. Gosh, they were cute. Twenty-seven-year-old Harvard grads."

Susan's heart sank. There was a reason she hadn't looked into this more in the past twenty-five years.

"Ah! And here. It says that there was one survivor of the accident. Major injuries." Lola's eyes were as wide as saucers. "Stan Ellis. He was in a coma for three weeks."

Chapter Twenty-Two

The following morning, Susan, Christine, and Lola woke up earlier than their father, just after five thirty, and sat out at the breakfast table with the diaries and letters in front of them. Susan was jittery and anxious and shot up for the kitchen to brew a pot of coffee and bake some biscuits in the oven. When they came out, Christine tore each individual piece from the layered biscuits one by one, analyzing them and muttering to herself. As a baker and a chef and everything in between, Susan imagined that the freezer-section biscuits didn't cut it in Christine's world. Still, nobody could eat. They were too nervous.

"I don't know why we're doing this," Lola suddenly blurted. "I mean, maybe he doesn't remember now? He has dementia, and it was all so long ago and now... Now at least we know that it wasn't him. That he wanted to keep Mom safe. He didn't keep the lights off the boat."

They heard the first creaks from the staircase. All their gazes shot toward the last step, where their father's left foot landed. Seconds later, his face appeared. He looked sleepy-eyed but happy, and his smile was immediate.

Despite all the lies over the years, all the silence, he still loved them more than ever.

"Look at my girls! All of you are such early risers," he beamed at them. "And you've already made breakfast? What did I do to deserve this?"

He moved toward the kitchen and poured himself a cup of coffee, an action the girls had watched him do time and time again over their childhood. Seeing it again like this felt like a stab in Susan's stomach. When he turned to join them at the breakfast table, he glanced down and then stopped short.

"What have you got there?" he asked, nodding toward the letters and diaries.

Lola sighed. "What do you think they are?"

Their father's eyes looked suddenly far away. "I haven't seen them in a really, really long time."

He tapped his coffee cup onto the table and sat across from the three of them. The soft morning light reflected across his handsome face, highlighting the wrinkles. He placed his hand across one of the diaries and shook his head. "Where did you find them?"

"In the attic," Susan responded. "We wanted to clean out more of Mom's stuff but then—"

Their father nodded. "I found the letters with her diaries a few months after Susan left for college. I didn't know what to do about them. I panicked and put everything in the attic. But it wasn't fair to you girls not to give you the letters. Everything had only just happened, and I didn't want to force you back into even more pain. We were all reeling. And—" He swallowed and thought for a moment. "What did they say?"

The sisters exchanged glances. Suddenly, Lola burst into tears and reached out to grab their father's hand over the diary. "Why didn't you tell us she was having an affair? Why didn't you tell us it wasn't your fault?"

The emotion seemed like a wave that smacked itself across Wes's face. He bowed his head and stared at Lola's hand over his for a long time. Susan felt heavy and strange, as though moving her arms and legs was no longer an option.

"I just couldn't," Wes murmured. "I couldn't allow all three of you to remember your mother like that. I loved her so much."

"Try because we've had a whole other idea in our heads for over twenty-five years. And we don't know how to grapple with this new reality," Christine said, her voice cracking.

"I didn't want to get a divorce," Wes said. His voice was very soft yet articulate. "I loved your mother since the day I met her. We were high school sweethearts. I thought we were going to take on the world together for the rest of our lives. But the inn ... parenting... all of it was so much work. I know that I wasn't as good of a husband to her as she was a wife to me. I regret that every single day of my life. Maybe, if I just would have been a little kinder, a little better, she wouldn't have strayed."

Susan felt each word like a punch to the stomach. She thought about Richard, about his own infidelities. Knowing that the mother she had given sainthood over the years had also done something so egregious was difficult to swallow. She now saw herself in the father she had always resented.

"But she just carried on this affair with you knowing about it? For a year?" Lola demanded.

"Maybe even two years. I don't know exactly when it started," Wes returned. He sipped his coffee, and his eyes were far away. "We'd known Stan for a long time. He came to the island when he was around thirty, I guess, and soon went up the ranks at that fishing company. Everyone talked about him like he was God's gift to fishing. And he was. I actually went with him a few times when you girls were younger. I had no qualms with him. And I certainly didn't know he had any interest in my Anna."

Here, he coughed and looked on the verge of choking up.

"The night she left, I knew she was going with Stan. All you girls were off somewhere."

Susan remembered. She had been off making out with Scott. She'd always been so angry with herself for this. How dare she do something so careless while her mom left the world forever?

"And I begged her to stay home," Wes continued. "It was the height of the season. June third. And we had so, so many tourists coming through that weekend. She said she really needed a break—a way to cool off. She said she wouldn't be out all night, which was something she had gotten into the habit of doing. Thankfully, you girls never noticed that." Wes sighed. "I didn't know what to do or how to keep her at home. All I knew was I thought if I fought harder and insisted we keep trying, she would find her way back to me.

"That night, just after ten, I got a call from this older guy, Marcus, who worked down at the lighthouse near where it happened. He said there'd been an accident and that they'd already pulled Anna, my Anna, out of the water. She was dead at the scene, as were these two other tourists. I got in the truck, and I raced all the way there. When I got there, she lay beneath a sheet, and they wouldn't let me see her, and they said they had to take her away. The night was a blur and so dark. There was no moon. I remember that. Just dark and cold, and I saw Stan there on the stretcher too. They told me he'd just fallen unconscious. I was so furious at that. I mean, the guy had just killed my wife, and I couldn't even beat him up. I ran into the water and screamed and screamed at the sky."

Susan remembered when he had returned that night — completely drenched and out of his mind.

No wonder. She would have been out of her mind too. How could anyone live through all that?

"But why did you make us think you were in the boat with her?" Lola demanded.

"I... I panicked," Wes explained. "Lola, you were only twelve years old. Twelve! I had no idea what to do with you. You couldn't sleep for three or four days until you completely strung yourself out with exhaustion and collapsed on the porch. Christine, you were always gone with your friends for the rest of the time you stayed on the island, and you were just a young thing, just a young teenager. Susan..." He turned heavy eyes toward her. "I don't blame you for leaving as quickly as you could. The mood around this house was horrible. But when you did leave, it tore my heart in two."

Susan let out a sob. She dropped her face forward into her hands, and her shoulders shook as she cried freely. Her father's sturdy hand found her shoulder and held on to her across the table, another anchor in this terrible, volatile life trying to give her some comfort.

"Even when we left and we didn't talk. And you didn't know when you would see us again," Christine murmured, breathless. "You still wanted us to have a pure memory of Mom. Make her look like the good guy."

Their father nodded. "I don't know. It was probably the wrong thing to do. I have gone the past twenty-five years feeling really, really unsure about everything in my life. The closest thing I've had to clarity, ironically, is right now. I was diagnosed with dementia, but I have my three girls here, and that is all that counts right now. And you finally know the truth."

It wasn't really clear what to do after all this. Nobody could eat. Christine brewed another pot of coffee that was largely ignored. Susan texted Natalie to make sure neither she nor Wes was needed at the inn that day. Ultimately, they decided to take out Wes's boat and motor around the Sound with a few bottles of wine, a picnic, and the stories of their mother that they wanted to share.

"She really couldn't get Susan to stop crying there for a while," Wes shared, midway through a glass of light rosé, his eyes happy yet distant. "You were maybe seven or eight months old. And she figured out the only song that made you perk up was—believe it or not—that theme song from *Ghostbusters*. I swear, for a full three months, that was the only song we ever played in this house. Whenever I hear it out in the world, I'm immediately taken back to those early days of fatherhood. Anna and I were more in love and more confused than ever in those days—being young parents and all. I think if I could relive any days, I would relive those."

"Gee. Thanks, Dad," Lola said with a smile.

"Nah. All the days. All the days with all my girls were perfect," Wes said, chuckling.

It was a perfect day, despite its pain. The sun crept down to tuck them back in, safe in the truth. As Susan lay awake that night, she felt the weight of her own secrets and the massive effect they could have on the ones she loved most.

Perhaps she would find the strength to speak.

Chapter Twenty-Three

A few days after Susan went to Scott's house and accused him of stealing from the Sunrise Cove Inn, Frampton Freight had a day off. Throughout the past years, Chuck and Scott liked to take at least one or two days off a month to regroup and recharge. Normally, Scott liked to take his boat out, go fishing, sit and think or even host his son on the island, depending on Kellan's schedule.

However, on this day off, Scott had a mission. He had returned to the Frampton Freight office, read through all the old receipts, old Excel sheets, and countless bits of paperwork, and deduced that Chuck Frampton had stolen over $40,000 from the Sunrise Cove Inn over the past eight months. The idea that all this had happened under Scott's nose chilled him to the bone. He had no idea how he would approach his brother, how he would explain all this to Susan, or how he could even fully face himself.

Regardless, he had the hard proof that this had

occurred, and he gathered all the evidence together in a folder and tucked it into the side pocket of the front seat of his truck. Then, he sat in the front of his truck for a long time; his hands wound tightly at the steering wheel as he blinked out at the gorgeous Nantucket Sound.

In the past few weeks, Susan Sheridan had returned to his life. It had felt like a smack to the face. He had been forced to reckon with the fact that, largely over the past few years, he'd wasted his life. He was only a phone-call father; his ex-wife didn't want anything to do with him, and he spent most of his nights alone at his house.

His closest friend, as of late, had been his brother, Chuck, since they spent so much time working together.

Now, Chuck felt like a stranger.

But Scott felt he needed answers before he did anything. He and Chuck had taken over Frampton Freight from their parents years ago. Maybe Chuck would listen to some kind of reason. Maybe he had the money in a savings account somewhere and could easily pay it back quietly. It wasn't like Chuck lived wildly outside his means. To Scott, Chuck's house was a little run-down one-story home.

Scott parked in Chuck's driveway. With his windows down, he could hear the baseball game that blared out from Chuck's living room. Chuck and Scott were both huge Baltimore Orioles fans since their dad had grown up in Maryland before moving to the island for their mom. They'd only been to a few games in their life, decades ago —but all those memories were just a blur. All his life, Scott had had a lot of trouble with his brother and all his strange and frantic qualities, his ability to bully and say horrible, cutting remarks. But back then, back when they'd been younger, Scott had really respected and loved his brother.

Scott knocked on the door. Every single bone in his body felt like rubber.

"Who is it?" Chuck hollered.

"It's me. It's Scott," Scott returned.

"Oh. Why'd you knock? Come in. It's the bottom of the third."

Scott entered the dusty little house. Chuck didn't even glance at him when he entered. Instead, he reached down into a little mini-fridge and passed Scott a beer. Scott took it but didn't open it. He remained standing, even as Chuck smacked his palms together and screamed at the screen. Scott had no idea what happened on TV. It could have been in a foreign language for all he knew.

"I know what you've been doing," Scott suddenly said.

Chuck didn't even glance at him. "Sit down, Scott. You're making me nervous. I have some chips in the pantry if you want them."

Scott didn't budge. He swallowed and said, "Chuck. Can you turn the TV off? I need to talk to you. It's urgent."

"Scott, come on. The Orioles are on. Are you sick or something?"

Finally, Scott burst toward the TV and smashed his finger against the power button. Immediately, the game went off. Chuck blinked his huge eyes at him, his jaw open.

"What's gotten into you?"

Scott placed his unopened beer on top of the TV. "You've been stealing from the Sunrise Cove Inn for the past eight months. I know everything. Forty thousand dollars. A little here, a little there, and suddenly, you have a hefty second wage, all to yourself. I know I haven't seen a single dime of that money."

Slowly, a smile inched its way across Chuck's face. "You say you have proof?"

Scott nodded. His hands formed fists as he studied his brother's evil face. "Just tell me. Tell me why you did it."

Chuck leaned down, opened the fridge, grabbed another beer, and popped it open with a flourish. He then stood and walked toward the window, with its beautiful view of the forested surroundings. "Why do you think I did it?"

Scott hated when Chuck played these stupid games. Chuck swung around and made heavy eye contact with him. Then, he shrugged. "What are you going to do about it, Scotty? Are you going to tell me I've been a very bad boy? You don't even know the half of it. I haven't only taken a few pennies here and there from the Sunrise Cove Inn. No. How many companies do we deliver to? Well, almost all of them have suited up my bank account quite nicely. Sunrise Cove Inn was just an easy target, what with Wes Sheridan's memory taking a hike."

"You will repay all that money, Chuck," Scott grumbled. "Mom and Dad didn't raise us to be like this."

"Oh? What did they raise us to be, then? Losers, like you? All alone in that shack you call a house, calling your little son on the phone and helping him with his math homework? Oh, I forgot. You also have this new fling with the woman who left you and almost immediately had a baby with another man. Twenty-five years ago," Chuck scoffed.

"I told you. We're just friends. We go back a long time," Scott insisted.

"So you're saying that you aren't having a fling, even though you spend all that time together? That's even sadder," Chuck said with a laugh.

Scott's brain boiled with rage. "That's it. I can't work with you. Never again. I'm out," Scott spat as his anger simmered even more.

"Great. I've waited for you to leave the company for years," Chuck retorted. "I hate driving in the truck with you. I hate hearing your stupid music. I hate when you talk about your stupid son."

Scott had never wanted to hit anyone more in his life. His fists tightened. "I will let everyone on the Vineyard know about you, Chuck. I will tell everyone that you're a liar and a thief, and I don't care what happens to me. These people on this island are good people. They've given us everything, and they've trusted us. And you've completely gone behind their backs."

Suddenly, Chuck dropped his head back and sucked down the rest of his beer. He then clamped his hand through the foil, smashing it, and tossed it into the corner. He leered at Scott for a second, then he turned, grabbed his wallet, his keys, and a little backpack, and disappeared out the front door.

Scott hustled toward the door to watch his older brother ease into the front of his truck and crank the engine. He barreled out the door, waving his arms. He had to stop him. But what then? He felt frozen with anger and resentment as his brother reared out of the driveway and then drove swiftly down the road.

Scott collapsed in his brother's porch swing and gasped for air. He rolled his fingers over his temple. He couldn't think properly. He needed to hash this all out with someone to know what to do next.

He had just learned a horrible secret, something that invalidated everything he'd thought he had known in his life.

And now, all he wanted to do was talk to Susan.

She would know what to do.

Chapter Twenty-Four

Susan, Lola, and Wes drove Christine to the ferry port that afternoon with heavy hearts. Christine had drunk a half bottle of wine at lunch and looked hazy-eyed and fearful. She'd confessed to Susan that she wasn't sure what she would return to in New York. Things with Frank had been frantic as the restaurant had shut down, but they'd had several conversations over the phone—ones that yanked her back, just to see if they could patch any of this back together.

"Besides. I'm a pastry chef," she had said. "I have to work. And New York has a million different jobs for that sort of thing. If I don't work, I don't know what my reality is. I'm not a wife or a mother or anyone special to anyone."

"That's not true," Lola and Susan had both snapped. "You're our sister."

"And we're not going to let so much time pass. Not again," Susan insisted. "Not now that we know the truth about Mom and Dad."

Christine had nodded sadly. All of them had

commented on how bizarre it was to know the truth about this. It felt as if a weight had been lifted, as though they could proceed with their lives differently and with fresh perspectives. Their love for their father felt different and less shadowed.

Christine hugged Susan the longest at the ferry port. "You brought us all back here. I have to admit, I thought you were crazy. But this trip totally changed my life."

Susan rubbed her back and blinked back tears. When she stepped back, Christine beamed at Susan, Wes, and Lola. The ferry blared its horn, a sign that it was nearly time to depart. She grabbed her suitcases. "Until next time, Team Sheridan. I love you forever."

When she disappeared, Wes wrapped his arm around Susan's shoulder and hugged her against him. They watched the ferry as it buzzed out across the waters. Lola took a phone call while they waited for the ferry to disappear. Susan listened to Lola set up an interview with another Boston artist in a week's time. Her heart sank.

Maybe the summer she'd planned for, with all of them there together, wasn't to be.

When Lola hung up the phone, though, she shrugged. "I'll just be gone for a few weeks. Don't worry. I plan on making it back. I'm having too much fun!"

Susan and Wes both laughed. Wes suggested they pick up steaks to grill out later that night after he spent a bit of time at the office. Lola said she wanted to work for a while at the main house, while Susan said she wanted to head out for a walk.

"You okay to go alone?" Lola asked her, a pen already sliced between her teeth and ready to be gnawed on.

"Oh yeah. I have a lot to go over," Susan said, tapping her temple. "But, they're mostly good thoughts."

Lola sighed. "I miss her already. I wish we could have convinced her to stay."

"I know. But she's a New Yorker now, I guess," Susan said. "Just because my life is over in Newark doesn't mean I can expect it from her."

Although Susan had initially thought she would just walk around the area by their house, she instead got into one of the inn cars and started to drive. The island wasn't a big one, and she found herself weaving and winding on the old roads she and Scott had taken as teenagers—always with the windows down and the radio blaring. Nothing about their lives had been difficult back then. They'd had each other, and they'd had the island and the water and the sun. They hadn't needed anything else.

To her surprise, Susan found herself easily back at her and Scott's favorite make-out spot at the Great Rock Bight, which was located in Chilmark. The land was owned by the MV Landbank Commission, which meant that nobody could ever build on it. She parked in a wooded parking area, her head flashing with memories of long-lost summer nights, and then headed down the little steep path toward the water. It was late June at this point, but not many tourists knew about Great Rock Bight, as they normally kept to Jaws Bridge.

The beach pointed westward and had been one of the best places for sunsets and long conversations and whispered secrets. Now, standing there alone on the beach with the salty breeze collecting her locks and whipping them over her cheeks, she exhaled and closed her eyes and tried her best to organize her mind. The days had been explosive.

Now, she had to figure out what came next.

She was a divorced woman with an ailing father. She

was still in the beginning stages of repairing her relationships with her sisters. She had a daughter on the way to the altar and a son with two adorable babies.

But she was ready to build something on the island for herself.

And she could do that either with or without Scott.

Of course, there was so much he didn't know.

Suddenly, she heard a voice lash through the wind. She froze and glanced at the sky. Was she losing her mind? Was the earth trying to talk to her?

But then, it came again.

"SUSAN!"

She turned quickly to find Scott Frampton himself walking down the beach toward her. Her heart leaped into her throat. Wasn't she supposed to be cripplingly angry at him?

But no. As he approached and his gorgeous eyes found hers, she knew with every ounce of her being that Scott Frampton would never wrong her or her family.

He loved her. It was the only constant in her life at the moment.

Scott Frampton loved her and wanted her back. Maybe he had always wanted her back, ever since she'd left him. Maybe they could stop wasting the time they had left.

Maybe.

They stared at each other for a long time. It felt as if there was too much to say, and they didn't know where to start.

Finally, Susan said, "How did you find me?"

"I stopped by your house. Lola said that you went out for a walk but that you took the car for some reason. I had a weird hunch you'd come out here." He scratched the back of his head, then gave a wry smile. "It's always where you wanted to come back in the old days."

"I'd almost forgotten all about it," Susan said as she looked at her palms.

"I guess you remember more than you think," Scott said. He swallowed and then shifted his weight. "I have to tell you that I went through everything you said. The receipts, the ledgers—everything. Chuck has been stealing from Sunrise Cove and so many other restaurants and businesses across the island. I cannot even begin to fathom the weight of what he's taken. It probably sounds nuts that I trusted him all these years. But—"

Susan reached out to grab his hand. Immediately, the tension in his body released. She stepped toward him, closing the distance. Their hands hung, locked together, between them. She studied his handsome face.

"It's okay, Scott. We'll figure it out," she whispered.

Scott furrowed his brow. "You didn't seem like that a few days ago. I thought you were going to rip my head off."

"So many things have changed since then, if you can believe it," she said.

As the waves crept over the shore, inching their way to Susan and Scott's feet, as the sun dipped toward the horizon line, Susan explained what she had learned about her mother's death: that she hadn't been with her father after all; that Stan had been the driver; that she'd had a two-year affair; that Wes had fought tooth and nail to try to keep their family together. It hadn't been enough—but that didn't negate all he had done.

"So we've been angry with him all these years for no reason," Susan finished. "And now, he's losing his memory, and the inn has lost all this money and... And I guess all I can do is try to make up for it by staying here and helping him and returning to my roots. I feel my mother here. I feel her in the sky and in the water and in every room of the house. But I also understand there's so much about my mother that I'll never really understand. My husband, he cheated on me. We'd been through so much together, and it was one of the most painful things I've ever gone through. My mother did the same thing."

Scott's eyes were heavy. His thumb smoothed over the top of her hand.

"But you can't spend your life blaming her for every-thing either," Scott said. "It's poison."

"I know."

They locked eyes for a long time.

"You were the only thing I could cling onto after she died. I was such a mess, and you were my anchor. And then I just—"

"It's okay," Scott said. "Don't linger on that, either. We're here now. We're together."

Suddenly, Susan fell forward and wrapped her arms tightly around him. His large hands fell over her back and eased across her shoulders. She let out a single sob and closed her eyes. He still smelled like his old self: like cedar and a subtle hint of cologne. She loved him more than she could bear.

All at once, his hand found the curve of her cheek, and his lips fell onto hers. It was the first kiss they'd shared since he'd left her at the ferry port over twenty-five years before, and it was urgent and overwhelming, the kind of kiss that could have knocked Susan to her knees if he hadn't had her all wrapped up in his arms.

When the kiss broke, Susan stepped back and dropped her arms to her sides. Shock rang through the air between them as the last of the orange and pink sunlight filtered across the waves.

"I've wanted to do that since I first saw you," Scott whispered as he searched her face.

Tears raced down Susan's cheeks now. It was too much. The lie. It had grown and grown, and now it felt like a block in the road between her and any kind of happy life she might have been allowed to have.

"I don't know if I can love you back in the way you want me to," she confessed.

Immediately, Scott looked as though she had stabbed him directly in the heart. His shoulders fell forward.

"I guess I should have expected something like this to happen. It was so much time. I don't know why I thought maybe we could have a second chance," he said.

"No. That's not it," Susan corrected. She closed her eyes tightly and willed herself to keep going. She hadn't articulated these words to anyone. Not Amanda. Not Jake. Not her sisters or her father or anyone she loved.

"If you want to love me, Scott, then you have to know the truth. You have to know that... I have had some pretty big health scares over the last year. I was diagnosed with stage two breast cancer last year," she explained. "And right now, I don't know about my future. I only know right now. Can you handle that?"

She expected Scott to demand more answers. It was his right. But instead of panicking, he stepped forward and wrapped his arms around her even tighter. She wavered on her knees but remained there, her cheek against his chest. His heart pounded with such certainty. She could have stayed there, listening to it for hours.

Scott and Susan sat out on the beach for a long time, their arms wrapped around each other. Scott asked her delicate questions about her diagnosis, about her mental state, about what she wanted in her life in the here in now, if she wasn't sure how much time she had.

"I didn't want to tell my sisters because I only just rekindled our friendship," Susan said. "I don't want them to think that I'm using them or trying to manipulate them into being in my life again. I had no idea how much I would fall back in love with all of this again. With the Vineyard. With my cousins and with the big house and with the Sunrise Cove Inn. The thought of going back to Newark is a painful one."

"I think your gut is telling you what you need to do," Scott said. "The gut is the only thing with sound logic in this world. I'm not a scientist, but even I know that's true."

Susan laughed and placed her head on his shoulder. "How did we miss out on so many years?"

"We didn't," Scott said. "We had all the years we needed apart. And now, we can have time together. We can watch as many sunsets on Great Rock Bight as you want."

"The tourists better not swarm it," Susan said. "This is our place."

They shared another kiss. Scott then suggested they head back to her place. Susan bolted upright in sudden memory: they had to do something about Chuck Frampton and his thousands and thousands of stolen cash.

"Do you think he'll run?" she asked.

"Maybe we should call the cops just in case," Scott said.

They returned to Scott's truck. Susan was underfed and exhausted and bleary-eyed and decided to pick up the Sunrise Cove Inn vehicle in the morning. Scott dialed the local police station in Oak Bluffs.

"Hey, Randy. This is Scott Frampton," Scott said.

Of course, Randy was another guy they'd gone to school with. The island was a densely layered photo album of memories come to life.

"Yeah, I actually have a report to make. I have good reason to believe that Chuck might be making his way off the island to escape from the law. I just learned that he's been stealing a good deal of money from a number of hospitality locations across the island and potentially beyond. Any chance you can get someone out to the ferry docks to check if he's on his way out?"

At first, Randy seemed confused. Scott explained again, this time a little slower with a bit more detail. Finally, Randy got off the phone.

"He's going to call me when they track down Chuck," Scott said. "I guess that's all we can do right now."

Susan scrubbed at her cheeks. "It feels like the entire world is upside down."

Scott took her hand and laced his fingers through it. "We're going to get through this together—all of it. I promise you."

Chapter Twenty-Five

Susan and Scott drove back to the main house. Neither of them spoke throughout the drive. The cool air shifted in through the opened windows and breezed past their faces. The radio played songs they had once loved and cried out to the skies above. The weight of time and life pressed hard against them now. Maybe it made them quiet, for now. There would be time to sing again, someday.

Back at the house, they found Lola on the porch writing notes to herself, still with that same pen between her teeth. She cast her gaze toward Scott and Susan, then scanned down to find their hands still locked together. Her grin widened.

"Oh, hello there. I see you found her," she said to Scott.

"I did! In our old secret place," Scott said.

"I guess I'm just that predictable," Susan said.

Scott and Susan explained what had been going on with Frampton Freight over the past eight months. Lola's brow furrowed, but she didn't act shocked. As a journalist,

Susan imagined that she'd seen much of the darkness of the world, just as Susan had. Still, you never expected this sort of thing to happen to you or the things you cared about.

"So, the police are going after him?" she asked.

"Yes. But there's a possibility he already left the island," Scott said. "I tried to call him a few minutes ago, but his phone is off. He's smarter than he looks. He might be difficult to catch."

Lola burst into action. She poured them each a glass of wine and ordered several pizzas.

"Both of you look like you haven't eaten anything today," she said. "And after all we've been through, I think we need a little nourishment."

They received word midway through dinner that Chuck had made his way off the island. Someone who knew him had spotted him at the ferry port in Falmouth. At the time, they'd just said hello and sent him on his way. After all, they were used to seeing Chuck Frampton all the time. He worked for the reputable company Frampton Freights. Why would anyone suspect him?

Over the next few days, it became clear to both Susan and Scott that Chuck might escape the situation altogether, although the police had alerted them that they'd sent out a warrant for his arrest and people were on the hunt for him. Susan knew it wasn't incredibly likely that he could just disappear forever. However, she didn't know how much cash he'd had saved up, potentially in an off-island location, awaiting him just in case this very thing happened.

She had seen villains before. She knew their games.

At first, Scott kept up his duties at Frampton Freight. He spent a great deal of those first few days explaining to all the members of the hospitality industry that he hadn't known his brother was a thief. There was a lot of talk of suing Frampton Freight, something that really affected Scott and kept him awake at night.

Only about a week after Susan and Scott renewed their relationship, Scott had vowed that he would continue to help clean up the inn with them. Wes's dementia was an ever-changing monster, with Susan recognizing little things he lost his way through nearly every day. She wanted to be there, just in case. And Scott was more than willing to be around. Plus, the house was big enough for Scott to stay with them a few nights a week if he chose to. It was always tempting with that stunning view of the water. Scott set to work revamping the house itself, just as he had with the inn: painting and fixing shutters and plotting out new projects for the rest of the year. Wes helped when he could and seemed pleased to do it, happy to lean again on his still-present strength and talk man-to-man with Scott, the only real "son-in-law" he had ever known.

Lola returned to Boston with a plan to be back on Martha's Vineyard in a few weeks. "I can work from anywhere. And like I said, not having Audrey around in the apartment is a bizarre thing. It makes me all jittery. Like I have no use anymore," she said.

So much had happened between the three Sheridan sisters over the past few weeks. Christine called every few days to report from New York. Apparently, she and Frank were in the last stages of closing up and clearing out the old restaurant. She had sent out several applications to work as a pastry chef across the city but hadn't received much interest. She sounded disheartened and, if Susan was honest, as though she had been drinking even more than normal. This worried her to no end, and she reminded herself to have a talk with Christine when she returned to the island.

When the pain struck her, Susan smoked her medical marijuana and leaned back on the porch swing, and let Scott hold her. Very rarely, she cried. She still hadn't been able to tell Amanda or Jake. In truth, she had hoped all this would just go away. It still could, she thought to herself. She knew that, and she held out hope for that surely sun-filled day when the Dr.s would tell her the surgery and the treatment had all actually worked, and she could go back to her old carefree existence.

When she was able to blot out the reality of her illness, however, Susan couldn't help but think these were the happiest days of her life. Every few mornings after he'd decided to stay the night, she awoke next to the love of her life, Scott Frampton. There was so much about him that was brand-new, fresh, and also so much about him that brought her back to beautiful memories. They talked almost constantly over dinner, telling tales from the years they had missed. Scott especially liked to hear stories about the years Susan had been a young mom.

"I was only nineteen when Jacob was born, and I had no idea what I was doing," she said, resting heavily on her hand as she gazed into Scott's eyes. "Richard was young, too, and he wasn't much help. I mean, can you imagine yourself at that age? You wouldn't have known what to do with a baby."

"Ah! An insult. I see what you're doing there," Scott said with a smile.

"That's not what I mean. Only that in this life, it seems like we jump into things without any real thought of what they'll do to us," she said. "And then we emerge as battered people. Every new decision tears us in two, and it's up to us to patch ourselves back together again."

"We're patching each other back again," Scott corrected her. "Bit by bit. I feel more and more whole than I did before you came back to the Vineyard."

Scott also told her bits and pieces of his life with his ex-wife and his son. "I worry that he won't know how to put me in his life since he lives so far away," he said. "I told him that we got back together, and he hardly knew about you. You're such a huge part of my past, and my memories, and my own flesh and blood didn't know. But I asked him if he might like to come out here during July to meet you and go fishing."

"That's fantastic!" Susan beamed. "I can't wait to meet him." She swallowed and added, "Is he anything like a typical teenage boy?"

Scott laughed. "Unfortunately, I think we have several more years of that."

Susan shrugged. "Such is life, I guess."

It was decided that Scott would sell Frampton Freights and focus entirely on the Sunrise Cove Inn. Susan asked him several times if that was what he really wanted to do, and each time he insisted he had no qualms about parting with his family's business. "Freighting is early work. It's tiring work. It's thankless."

At the inn, Wes, Susan, and Scott seemed to work as a united force together. With Chuck not stealing from them any longer, the inn flourished and was even featured in a *New York Times* article about "hidden gems across the country." Lola freaked out about that. "The TIMES?" she had said. "Man. I didn't think you guys would get published in the Times before I did."

By early July, there had been no sign of Chuck.

Since most of the hospitality sector had good insurance, they were able to get a lot of the stolen funds back. A newcomer to the island took on Frampton Freights, and Scott started full-time at the Sunrise Cove Inn. Every morning, Susan and Scott sat outside her father's office at the inn and shared a croissant and a pot of coffee before the rest of the hotel woke up. They were beautiful mornings, maybe some of the most beautiful of her life.

"I always thought sunsets on the island were my favorite," she said the morning of the Fourth of July. "But I've really come to appreciate sunrises with you."

Now that the Sheridan sisters had learned the truth of their mother's death, they sometimes spoke about what to do about Stan Ellis.

After all, he had been the one not to turn on the lights of the boat, causing the crash.

He had been the one who had tried to split up their family.

He was their childhood trauma, the monster that lurked beneath the bed.

When Susan asked Scott about him, he said that nobody really knew where Stan lived anymore, that he had moved to a very rural location on the island almost immediately after the accident. Sometimes, people saw him drinking at some of the bars across Oak Bluffs and Edgartown, but he kept to himself and didn't bother anyone.

On the afternoon of the Fourth of July, Susan stopped by Claire's flower shop to buy a bouquet of lilies. Lola was on her way to the island again, and she wanted to spruce up the place before her arrival. As Claire passed her the bouquet, Susan told her in hushed tones what she had learned about her father and Stan and their mother. Claire looked stricken.

"I can't believe everyone has kept such a big secret for so long," she said. "However, that does explain the incident that happened a few years ago."

Susan arched her brow. "What incident are you talking about?"

Claire's face looked shadowed, as though she immediately regretted mentioning it. She placed her hands on her hips and eyed the ground. "Uncle Wes met Stan Ellis at some bar, and there was some kind of altercation. Uncle Wes had a black eye for a long time. Mom was really upset. To me, it just seemed like typical island gossip and drama. But obviously, it was way more than that."

"Wow." Susan had never seen her father be violent with anyone. It was difficult to imagine him picking a fight with Stan. "You don't know where Stan lives, do you?"

Claire shook her head sadly. "Nope. I don't know if anyone else does either. He's kind of a ghost on this island, and honestly, I think everyone likes it like that."

Susan and Scott held a Fourth of July celebration at their house. Like other days, almost every single person from Susan's extended family came, including Aunt Kerry and Uncle Trevor, all their kids and grandkids, and even Susan's dearest friends, Lily and Sarah, who had worked their way easily back into Susan's life. They enjoyed weekly wine nights together, laughing and talking until midnight or sometimes later, which always left Susan bleary-eyed but happy at the inn the following day.

Lola arrived at the party just after eight, a beautiful and cosmopolitan thing who whipped off her sunglasses and called to her family and friends, "I'm back! The real party can begin!"

Susan was also terribly happy to welcome Scott's son, Kellan, for the Fourth of July. He was quiet and good-natured, with occasional jokes that made Susan burst into laughter. To her surprise, Kellan and Wes seemed to hit it off instantly. Now, as the fireworks began their tireless parade across the Nantucket Sound, Wes and Kellan sat near each other, exchanging stories.

Scott wrapped his arms around Susan from behind and whispered in her ear. "Look at all these people who love you. All of them are here for you today."

Susan chuckled. "I think they're here because I served them burgers, and there's a good view of the fireworks."

"You know how much you're loved, Susan Sheridan. The island got an extra jolt of life when you came back," Scott murmured, dotting a kiss on her cheek.

Fourth of July fireworks crafted a gorgeous collage of colors across the night sky over the next hour. Everyone gazed, stunned, bellies filled and heads spinning with joy and a tiny bit of alcohol. There was a perpetual childlike delight to the Fourth of July holiday, which Susan was eternally grateful for.

There was no telling what would happen next in her life. But she told herself to be grateful for the here and now. It was all they had. And there was enough love there to go around.

Epilogue

The wind whistled through the cracked windows and swirled across Susan's cheeks. Her eyelashes fluttered as she shifted from the dream world to reality. For a moment, she hadn't a clue where she was, only that she felt soft and cozy, loved in a way she hadn't been loved in a long, long time.

The rain pattered across the windowpanes. She opened her eyes to peer up at a still-unfamiliar ceiling. Her body was wrapped in a scratchy green blanket, and her dark hair was a chaotic mess across a large white pillow.

Of course, she had slept over at Scott's place.

She turned to the side to find that Scott was no longer in the sturdy place where he'd slept beside her. He'd kept a hand across her waist throughout the long, dark hours, always in contact. Sometimes, when she shifted in sleep—occasionally drifting into nightmares about her breast cancer diagnosis, about having to explain it to her daughter, Amanda, about her father's dementia—he dotted a kiss on her back, an assurance that she wasn't so lost; she had someone to cling to. A solace in the midst of the storm.

Susan lifted from the pillows and blinked around the small room, one of two in a tiny cabin at the very edge of the water. When Scott had first brought her to the little place, she'd felt a bit heartbroken. For years, she had channeled so much of her effort into creating a homey environment for herself, for Richard, and for their children. All the while, Scott had lived in a relatively small home.

He had seen this in her eyes: this sadness. He'd shrugged it off. "I've been a bachelor. This is all I've needed. And look at that view."

It was true that his view out the kitchen window of the Sound was remarkable. Susan rose to blink out at the waves, which tossed in the suddenly tumultuous midsummer weather. Scott had brewed a pot of coffee but had seemingly only drank a tiny bit. The bathroom door remained wide open, proof that Scott was nowhere to be found within the cabin itself.

Where had he gone? And why had he left her in the cabin alone?

Susan poured herself a piping hot cup of coffee and furrowed her brow. Had Scott mentioned anything regarding an appointment that morning? They'd spent the evening together, laughing and chatting about the beautiful Fourth of July celebration they'd had a few nights before. It had been remarkable to meet Kellan, Scott's son. Susan had felt this beautiful opening-up feeling, as though this first sight of Kellan would be one of many. Her inner psyche had whispered, *You're going to know this kid for a long, long time. You're going to watch him grow and change. And although you'll never love him the same way you love Amanda and Jake, you're going to build something else with him. Something that will last and have a power of its own.*

Scott Frampton, her high school sweetheart. Now, potentially the love of the second half of her life.

It was remarkable. It seemed outside of reality.

Susan couldn't have planned it better—and she was one of the better planners she knew.

At this moment, she noticed something on the little rickety kitchen table. It was an envelope on which Scott had written Susan, in his ever-familiar handwriting, which she remembered from flirty notes back in high school. Her heart pounded as she reached for the envelope and tore it open.

Good morning, beautiful,

I wanted to wake you, but you looked so beautiful sleeping there in my bed.

I can't begin to describe just how much I've wanted you in that bed since I first saw you swimming outside my cabin a few weeks ago. I've dreamed of it. I don't know what I did to deserve this goodness, but I thank God every day for it.

Being with you during this time has called to mind countless memories—times we shared together that, in all honesty, I never thought I would think of again.

So I've put together a bit of a game for you, darling.

Don't worry. I've asked Natalie to cover your shift at the Inn. She was happy to play along.

I know you tend to skepticism. I know you want to protest. I know you think games are a waste of time.

But I promise you. This one will be worth it.

Now: here's your first clue.

The year was 1991.

I caught your eye through the window of this cute little establishment.

You had vanilla ice cream on your nose.

When I teased you, you told me never to talk to you again.

I knew you didn't mean it.

See you when I see you.

Love,

Scott

Susan's smile widened as she folded up the little slip of paper. She remembered the day perfectly. She'd been fifteen years old, seated with Lily and Sarah at the little ice creamery in Edgartown. Already, she and Scott had been "on-again, off-again." At this point, however, Susan had recently told Scott that she wanted to date someone else.

"You dumped Scott Frampton?" Lily had asked brightly over ice cream. Her tongue had been covered in green mint ice cream.

Susan had shrugged and dug into her ice cream. "It's not like we were going to get married or something."

"But he loved you so much!" Lily had cried. "He told someone in gym class that he wants you to have his kids."

Susan had scrunched her nose at this. "I'm fifteen years old. And besides, Josh is hot, and I really want to kiss him after school tomorrow. He said that we could meet by the pier and get milkshakes."

Lily and Sarah had exchanged exasperated glances. Susan—who, admittedly, had been quite frightened at the prospect of dating the super-jock, Josh—kept eating her ice cream as though none of this bothered her.

"I just want to have as many experiences as I can," Susan had explained.

"Did he seem upset?" Sarah had asked.

Susan had furrowed her brow. "No."

This, in truth, had bothered her even more. In fact, when Susan had explained that she wanted to date other people, Scott Frampton had actually laughed. "Right. Like you'll find another relationship like this one. Good luck to you," he'd said.

This had been a level of arrogance that Susan had detested.

Still, it had given her pause.

Had she made a huge mistake?

The forty-four-year-old Susan decided to play along with Scott's game. She styled her hair and slipped into a dress she'd brought to wear for the day. After a quick gloss of makeup, she hustled through the rain to her car and cranked the engine. The windshield wipers swept side-to-side to whip off the droplets. In moments, she shot toward Edgartown, toward the ice creamery.

As she drove, more memories of that day sizzled through her.

As she'd sat, talking about the breakup with Scott, she'd felt someone's gaze through the window and looked up to find him smirking at her. He'd had fishing supplies with him; Chuck had lurked somewhere behind, packing up their truck after a full day's boat ride. Susan's stomach had dropped out from under her. Before she'd known what she did, she shot up from the stool and stormed out of the ice creamery. Her ice cream flailed around in her hand.

"What are you doing here, Scott?" she'd demanded outside on the sidewalk. "I told you I didn't want to see you anymore, and now, you're stalking me? This is ridiculous. You're so obsessed."

The ridiculous things teenagers say and think, Susan thought now as she drove.

"Wow. What kind of arrogance does it take to think that just because we ran into one another here, I stalked you here?" Scott had said, a smile tweaking up between his cheeks.

"I'm just trying to have an ice cream with my friends," Susan had shot back.

Scott's eyes had connected with hers. There had been such fire behind them. Susan could feel it: even though he'd said she wouldn't find another relationship like the one they had—he still loved her. He loved her with every fiber of his being. He wanted no one else.

"How's it going with Josh?" he'd asked.

Susan had flared her nostrils. "Fine. I mean, none of your business."

Scott had chuckled at this. He'd stepped toward her, too close—so close that she thought he was going to kiss her.

And, in fact, she would have welcomed it.

For in these moments, Susan knew what a complete imbecile she'd been.

She loved Scott just as much as he loved her.

Maybe she even loved him more.

But just as she'd thought he would kiss her, he reached down and smeared his thumb against her nose, removing a huge droplet of ice cream.

She'd been mortified.

"Clean yourself up, Sheridan," Scott had said coyly. "Call me when you get Josh out of your system. Maybe I'll be available. Maybe not."

The memory, of course, made Susan laugh now. She parked outside the ice creamery and blinked at the window, at the stool on which she'd sat when she'd first spotted him. All of it looked exactly the same as it had some twenty-seven years before. It was enough to break her heart.

It was early—but tourists tended to eat ice cream at any time of day on Martha's Vineyard. The bell jangled as Susan entered the little ice creamery, and the teenager who wore braces greeted her from behind the counter.

"Hi there," Susan said, beaming. "This is going to sound crazy, but do you happen to have anything here for a Susan Sheridan?"

The girl smiled. "Yes! I've had no idea why this is here."

The girl whipped around, disappeared into the back room, and then reappeared with a basketball. Scott had written, "To give to Susan Sheridan" in big block letters on a note attached to the ball itself. When Susan tore the note off, however, there was no clue.

"I guess the basketball is the clue?" Susan marveled.

The girl shrugged. "Pretty weird."

Susan laughed. "Do you mind if I grab a cone while I think? I have to go through a lot of memories in my head. Sugar might help."

"Sugar helps with everything," the girl agreed.

Susan ordered a small mint chocolate chip cone, a callback to Lily's, and spun the basketball around and around on the counter near the window. She sat on the same stool from the past. What did this clue mean, exactly? Where did Scott want her to go next?

There was the high school basketball arena. That was a possibility—although Susan couldn't remember any overly personal memories there.

There had also been a little basketball court at the

church—but she and Scott had never spent much time there together since his family had gone to another church.

With a lick of the ice cream, a memory shot through her.

If anything, this had to be it.

There had been a little paved court a few blocks from their high school.

At age sixteen, they'd gone there together several times to shoot hoops and get away from tourists. Back then, even though they'd loved summer, it had always been irritating at the beginning of summer, as their favorite beaches and hideaways had been taken over.

On one particular steamy summer afternoon, Susan had grown irritated with Scott. She couldn't fully remember why. Again, it had probably involved another guy who'd crushed on her—the potential of another life. At sixteen, it wasn't as if she was entirely settled.

"I think maybe we should see other people," she'd said again, the basketball in her hand.

Again, Scott had smirked at her. "Why's that?"

"I just worry we're not living as much as we should be," she'd returned.

"Do you wish I was someone else?" Scott had asked. "Wish I had a different hair color? Wish I was better at math?"

Susan had rolled her eyes.

"No. You don't. You know we're perfect for each other," Scott had shot back.

"But what if we're not?" Susan had said.

"I don't know. I don't really care to find out," Scott had said.

Susan had begun to dribble the ball. Since they'd

frequently played that spring, she'd gotten pretty good at it. Suddenly, Scott whipped toward her, stole the ball, and smashed it through the hoop.

"Asshole," Susan had muttered.

"If you want to leave me so bad, why don't you play me?" Scott had said. "If you win, you can date someone else. If I win, we have to work it out."

Susan had furrowed her brow. Arrogance and confidence had sizzled through her. There was no way she would allow Scott Frampton to beat her. Sure, he was taller, stronger—but she was more stubborn.

"Deal," she'd said.

The game had ravaged on for a long time. For the first half hour or so, Susan flung herself around that stupid court on a kind of mission. But as time trickled forward, she'd found herself laughing, teasing Scott, occasionally jumping on his back and holding him so that he couldn't make a basket.

Ultimately, the two of them had fallen into each other's arms and made love in Scott's truck.

Scott had teased her. "I told you. I knew you wouldn't be able to leave me."

At this, Susan had laughed and told him to clean up his act. "I'm always on the brink of breaking your heart."

Susan drove back toward Oak Bluffs, easily winding her way toward that basketball court. The pavement looked like it hadn't been redone in twenty-five years. She spotted a little card taped to the pole as she walked toward the basketball hoop. Again, Scott had scrawled her name on it.

Susan tore open the envelope.

Congratulations! That was a tough one, and you figured it out.

I guess I shouldn't be surprised. You were always the smarter one of the two of us.

You always told me you would break my heart—and you did.

It's not that I didn't believe you. It's only that I wanted as much time with you as I could get, before you went off and became the great Susan Sheridan I always knew you would be.

Behind the little card was a DVD.

Susan frowned. The note had nothing else on it—so obviously, the clue was tied up in the DVD.

The DVD itself was *Pretty Woman*.

Naturally, it had been a movie Susan and her sisters had watched over and over again as teenagers. They'd loved it. Susan had tried and failed to make her hair like Julia's—big and bouncy. Although it was rather big and rather bouncy, it had never reached Julia Roberts's goodness.

But why had Scott included *Pretty Woman* as a clue?

Susan turned around and blinked out toward the road. She placed the DVD against the skin of her upper chest. It had quit raining, but the clouds still billowed overhead.

Julia Roberts. Richard Gere.

What had any of this to do with—

Oh!

The thought smacked Susan against the head.

Early September 1993.

Susan's mother had been dead for a few months.

She and Scott had sat out in the still-lingering summertime heat, watching the sailboats as they skidded across the horizon. During this time, Susan had occasionally dipped into bouts of serious sadness, and Scott had

211

really struggled to bring her out of them. He'd tried everything. Jokes. Silly songs. Candy bars, dinners out, boat rides. Sometimes, these things yanked her from her fog, but other times, they only reminded her of the "before" and the "after." In her eyes, she'd been so much bigger before her mother's death.

Scott had splayed his arm over her back and held her close to him. He'd occasionally tried on different words, any attempt to engage her. She'd hardly heard him.

Scott had told her he would be right back. He disappeared to his truck. In the haze of the silence, Susan had felt monstrously sad, as though the wave of grief had crashed over her and cast her under. She'd found it difficult to breathe.

And she'd hardly heard the woman asking for directions.

"Excuse me? I'm so sorry to interrupt," the woman had said brightly.

Susan had blinked up, hardly able to register anyone else's syllables. "What was that?" she'd asked clumsily.

The woman had the biggest smile she'd ever seen. She looked so happy, like the personification of a summer's day. She wore a gorgeous strappy red dress and looked suntanned and free.

"I just was curious if you could point me in the direction of the Joseph Sylvia State Beach?" the woman asked. "I think I'm a little turned around."

Ah. Another tourist. Susan had sighed. "It's just over there. About a quarter of a mile. If you keep walking along it, you'll find the bridge where they filmed that famous scene in Jaws."

"That's such a good tip. Thanks." The woman had a

vague southern accent. She certainly wasn't from around there.

"Do you need anything else?" Susan had asked her blindly.

The woman had shaken her head. Her curls had tossed around with the shake. She really was the most beautiful woman Susan had seen up close. She should be famous, was actually something Susan had thought at the time.

At that moment, Scott had appeared behind the bench. Susan had turned back to see him, bug-eyed as if he'd just seen a ghost.

"Hi there," Scott had said to the woman.

"Hi. I just got some directions. Thanks again. You guys enjoy the rest of your day. It's a beautiful one," the woman had said. She then turned, tossing her curls, and marched in the direction Susan had told her to go.

When she was safely out of earshot, Scott had blurted, "Oh my god! You must be going nuts!"

Susan had arched her brow as Scott had sat beside her. "Why?"

"Because..."

"Because why?"

"You really didn't recognize that woman?" Scott had asked.

Susan had shrugged. "She seems nice. Certainly beautiful. I don't know."

"She was Julia Roberts!" Scott had cried.

In that moment, Susan had felt the truth of it like a sinking sensation in her gut. She'd placed her hands on her cheeks in surprise. "No. I can't believe I just..."

"And you didn't even notice!"

"I just thought she was some random lady."

Scott had burst into laughter. "That's literally one of the only people you have ever told me you wanted to meet —and you didn't even recognize her."

Susan had blushed, then burst into laughter. She hadn't laughed in many weeks, and it hurt her stomach and cheeks. Her eyes filled with tears, but they were happy ones.

"This is ridiculous," she'd said, swiping tears away from her cheeks. "I can't believe it."

Now, Susan made her way to that very bench. She felt as though she walked a strange line between past and future as she went, as though she could literally feel teenage Scott and teenage Susan around her, walking down these very streets and eating ice cream and stealing vodka and swimming in the Sound. What a reckless, beautiful time it all had been—and Scott had been right to force her down this path.

When she reached the bench, she found another note. But as she tore it open, she spotted Lola coming toward her. Her gorgeous bohemian dress swirled around her thighs, and her hair was caught up in the wind and tossed back. Susan felt another jolt of happiness. She was so grateful that Lola had asked to do more freelance jobs so that she didn't have to return to Boston right away.

Secretly, Susan harbored the idea that she and Lola would remain on the island for quite some time. If they could yank Christine back from New York, all the better.

"What have you been up to all day?" Lola cried as she approached.

Susan fluttered the letter from Scott through the air. "To be honest, I'm on a kind of journey. Scott has a whole scavenger hunt laid out for me. Literally memory lane."

Lola arched her brow. "He always loved you a little too much, didn't he?"

"I'll take it now. Feels like maybe I took him for granted when we were younger."

"We took everything for granted back then," Lola returned.

"That's true."

The sisters regarded one another for a moment. Lola shifted her head toward the Sunrise Cove Inn, located just about a quarter mile away in the opposite direction of the Joseph Sylvia Beach.

"It's about lunchtime, and I'm famished. Do you want to join me for a salad and a glass of wine?" Lola asked.

"I thought you'd never ask," Susan said, slipping the note from the bench into her back pocket. There was no telling how long this scavenger hunt would go on—and she was fully prepared to milk it as long as she could. She loved living in these memories.

The sisters walked back toward the Sunrise Cove. Susan explained the places she'd been so far on her scavenger hunt—the ice creamery, the basketball court, the DVD.

"He's so creative!" Lola cried with a twinkle in her eye.

When they sat at the familiar table on the far end of the bistro, one of the busboys, Ronnie, approached to say hello. He placed his hands on his hips. "I can't keep you sisters apart. Susan? Lola? Is Christine about to come through those doors too?"

Lola chuckled. "We wish. Hey, do you want to suit us with some specialty salads with blue cheese and smoked salmon?"

"Oh, yes. Sounds great," Susan affirmed.

"Maybe two glasses of chardonnay as well," Lola said.

Ronnie nodded and turned back toward the server, who stood in conversation with the main chef, Zach. Susan remembered that Zach and Christine had always had a beef in high school.

"Do you remember why Zach and Christine didn't get along?" she asked Lola now.

Lola furrowed her brow. "Christine always had a bone to pick with people. There's no telling what Zach did wrong."

"Let's ask him!" Susan said suddenly.

"If Christine found out that you did that..."

But already, Susan waved to bring Zach closer to the table. Zach beamed at the sisters as he approached. Susan had to admit: he was still just as handsome as he'd ever been. Was he arrogant about it? Was that something Christine had decided was enough to pin her hate on?

"Good afternoon, ladies," Zach said. "Ronnie tells me you're interested in our specialty salads? Would you like anything else?"

"Just curious about something," Susan said.

"What's up?"

"Why do you and Christine hate each other?"

Zach guffawed, clearly surprised. He flashed his eyes out toward the horizon line across the Sound.

"I don't think she'd be entirely happy if I told you the story," Zach said finally.

Lola and Susan exchanged glances. Lola's grin widened.

"So it was kind of a big deal?" Lola said.

"I guess. Or not. I don't know. Everything's a big deal when you're a teenager, right?" Zach said. He palmed his neck, looking strangely nervous.

"I am so curious," Susan marveled.

"I'm sure she doesn't think about it. We're all so much older now," Zach affirmed. "We've lived lives since then."

Lola and Susan exchanged glances again.

"You'd be surprised what we remember," Susan said, considering the day she'd just had.

"You sound cryptic," Zach said with a laugh. "Did Christine mention something to you?"

"No. She's still safe and sound in New York," Susan said.

"For now," Lola offered, arching her brow.

"What's that supposed to mean?" Zach said. He looked strangely nervous. "Did she mention something about leaving that restaurant gig? I've read up about it before. Chez Frank. They do fantastic business. I would love to pick her brain about it sometime."

"The next time she's on the island, we'll send her your way," Lola said. "Just don't blame us if she bites your head off."

Their salads arrived. Lola and Susan fell into easy conversation about a recent piece Lola was writing about an artist in Boston.

"How's Audrey's internship going in Chicago, by the way?" Susan asked, sipping her wine.

"I think she really likes it," Lola said, beaming. She collected her hands beneath her chin. "I have a feeling about this girl. I messed up, you know? I fell in with the wrong crowd a few times. Heck, I had a kid at nineteen."

"So did I," Susan said with a smile. "But look how we turned out?"

"Christine is maybe the most impressive of the three of us," Lola affirmed. "She's studied pastry making in so many major cities. London, Paris, Stockholm..."

Susan pondered this for a moment. "I wish it would have made her happier."

"Me too."

"I wish there was a way we could bring her back here with us," Susan said.

"But I just don't know if it could make her happy after so many years in New York," Lola offered. "How can she go back to eating dinner with us every night after hobnobbing with celebrities in Manhattan?"

"You suggesting we aren't good enough?" Susan asked with a wide grin.

"That's exactly it," Lola returned.

As they neared the end of the lunch, Susan felt tugged back to the note card Scott had left her. She dotted her napkin across her lips. "I think I'd better get back to my scavenger hunt."

"I understand," Lola said.

"You up to much the rest of the afternoon?" Susan rose and gathered her purse and whipped her hair behind her back.

Lola considered this. "I'm not really sure."

"What do you mean?"

"Well, I haven't figured out a way to tell you yet."

"Tell me what?"

Lola gave her a mischievous smile.

"What is going on?" Susan demanded.

Lola shrugged. "I have your next clue."

Susan arched her brow. "No, you don't."

"Why won't you believe me?"

"I just know that I already have it." Susan grabbed the envelope from her purse and waved it. "It's right here. I got it from the bench."

Clearly, Lola was confused. It was the only solution.

But Lola just said, "Open it."

Susan heaved a sigh, sneaked her finger into the envelope, then ripped it open. She tugged the note card out and read the words:

Listen to Lola.

Susan returned her gaze to Lola. Her cheeks were hot. "No. Way. You were in on it the whole time?"

Lola giggled. "I will never give everything away. Only what I've been told to give."

"I can't believe it. Even my family has ganged up on me, now," Susan said. "So come on. Tell me. What's my clue? I'm getting anxious to keep going."

Lola rose and led Susan back into the afternoon. The clouds had begun to clear, revealing a gorgeous eggshell blue sky beneath.

"Okay. The year was—I believe—1992," Lola began. "That's what Scott says, so I have to believe him. I was just a little kid."

"Right."

"But I decided to go on a hike by myself because I got into a fight with my best friend about something," Lola continued. "And I was going through Felix Neck, whistling and looking at birds and minding my own business, when suddenly—"

Susan's lips formed a round O. She stopped walking and blinked wide eyes toward her younger sister.

"You found us when we were about to..."

"Yep," Lola affirmed. "It almost traumatized me! But you convinced me that you were just changing into your swimsuit or something."

Susan cackled. "I can't believe he remembers that!"

"I can't believe I lived through that trauma," Lola corrected.

"So the next clue is down by that little clearing. We used to go there all the time in the spring before the tourists came," Susan said.

"Disgusting," Lola said. "I can't believe you teenagers."

"Not like you weren't up to your own mischief after I left," Susan said.

Immediately after she said this, of course, her heart flooded with sadness. She did regret leaving Lola and Christine behind—falling immediately in line with Richard and popping out a few babies. It had been a different time. There'd been so much pain.

They couldn't linger on it now.

Together, Lola and Susan hiked through Felix Neck on the hunt for this little clearing. As they walked, they compared notes on what it had been like to raise Audrey and Amanda.

"Amanda was so much like me, so I always had a hunch what she was really up to," Susan said, chuckling.

"You think she snuck around with boys?" Lola asked.

"Sure. But I always could trust her to get her home-work done and always use protection, that kind of thing," Susan said. "She was responsible, almost to a fault."

"Like you!" Lola cried.

"Something like that," Susan affirmed. "What about Audrey?"

"She was a menace," Lola said.

"Like you!"

"Ha. I felt like I always had to get her out of trouble. She got busted for drinking a few times. She ran around with a few jocks who broke her heart..."

"Also something you did," Susan said.

"Hey! They never broke my heart," Lola said. "They only tugged me around a little bit. Bruised me up."

"Right."

"Still, raising a daughter was such a struggle," Lola continued. "I always knew what she was up against. A whole world of bad men—men who wanted to use her or talk down to her. I'd been through it and knew she was always headed toward it. I can only hope that it's gotten better in twenty years..."

"But I doubt it," Susan said with a sigh.

"Me too, unfortunately," Lola said.

The sisters walked together in silence for a while, both stewing in what they'd uncovered about their similar views of the world as perceived as women. The hike was a rather long one, something Susan had forgotten about. She supposed that back when they'd been teenagers, she and Scott had been much more lithe and powerful, with unlimited energy.

As they neared the little clearing, Susan's mind spun round and round with memories of those hot-hot-hot summer nights with her high school lover. It was funny looking back at those feelings as a forty-four-year-old. Had she ever had such feelings for her husband, Richard? She remembered her first time with Richard like, "Was that really it?" Still, she remembered thinking that maybe, as you grew up and grew older, passion wasn't as much a part of everything.

Goodness, she'd been so wrong.

When they reached the little clearing, Susan and Lola stood with their hands on their hips and scanned the little area.

"Does it bring back all those memories?" Lola asked.

"Don't start, Lorraine," Susan returned.

"I can see it. You're swimming in all those high school memories..."

"Ugh. I don't see a note anywhere. Are you sure that Scott told you the right clue?"

Lola cast Susan a playfully dark look. "Are you suggesting that I got it wrong?"

"You are the youngest," Susan pointed out.

"That's so a thing an older sister would say," Lola said.

Suddenly, there was a voice between the trees.

"Do you guys ever quit fighting?"

Susan's heart beat wildly as her daughter stepped out from between the trees. She held a balloon string between two fingers and guided the bright blue orb above her toward the center of the clearing. Susan could never get enough of looking at her daughter's beautiful face, her certain eyes, her gleaming smile. Sometimes, when she spotted her, she thought, *Is it possible that I really brought her into the world? Me?*

Of course, then she had to remind herself that Richard had had something to do with it, too—although Amanda had increasingly insisted that Richard was only five percent of her personality, and she wasn't very keen on that part.

"What are you doing here!" Susan cried. Dancing forward, she draped her arms around her daughter and cradled her close.

"Don't let me lose this stupid balloon," Amanda said, chuckling. "I was told to stand here at three o'clock in the afternoon and wait for you to arrive. But it's almost four! I've been out here for ages, and I really have to pee!"

"Scott's roped all of you into his game, hasn't he,"

Susan said. She gripped the balloon string and blinked up at it. "I guess this is the next clue?"

"Yes." Amanda frowned. "But what is this all for, anyway, Mom? I don't get it."

"Me neither. Scott's asked that I go along with it."

"That goes against everything in your nature. You never just go along with anything," Amanda said.

"Maybe it's time I try," Susan said with a shrug.

She then tugged the balloon down toward her and popped it with a firm, manicured nail. Suddenly, a little tiara, covered in jewels, tumbled out of the balloon and fell to the ground at their feet. Susan felt a stab of recognition.

"Oh my gosh," Lola blared. "Is that...?"

Susan crept down and grabbed the edge of the tiara. She lifted it into the sunlight. "I thought I'd never see this thing again."

"What is it?" Amanda asked.

Susan's heart thudded. "It's the crown I got when Scott and I were named prom king and queen."

"Mom! You never told me you were prom queen," Amanda said.

"I guess I wanted to forget it," Susan whispered.

"Wow. That is kitschy, isn't it?" Lola said. She grasped the crown and tilted it, investigating the shoddy red jewels.

"Don't belittle my crown," Susan said with a dry laugh. "I was proud to be prom queen."

"Your senior year?" Amanda asked.

"Yep."

"So after Grandma's accident."

"Yes," Susan and Lola answered at once.

Lola sniffed. After a pause, she said, "I remember

watching you get ready for prom with Lily and Sarah in your bedroom. You all looked like princesses to me. I was, what, twelve? I felt like being a teenager was a million years away. But oh gosh, Susan, remember? You put makeup on me before you left. It was the first time I ever wore lipstick."

"I remember that. Dad nearly freaked when he saw you. He was like—she's only eleven! And then I had to remind him that, actually, you were twelve."

"Dad was going through a lot," Lola affirmed. "I'm sure he had no idea what to do with any of us."

"But why did Scott have your crown?" Amanda asked.

Susan bit hard on her lower lip. "Because I threw it at him."

Both Lola and Amanda shrieked with shock.

"That night?" Lola demanded.

"Yes," Susan said. She eased toward the side of the clearing and sat on a cleared stump. She felt hazy from the memory. "Prom was early May. I'd just decided to leave the Vineyard and head off to school. Until then, I'd kept Scott at a distance, trying to decide what I wanted to do. That night, a bit drunk at an after-party, we sat outside and kissed beneath the moon. I knew I loved him more than I could ever love anyone. I also knew I had to leave him."

"So you told him there. At this person's house," Amanda confirmed.

"No. He suggested we walk back to my house," Susan said quietly. The memory felt like a knife through the stomach. "He was good at reading what I needed. And he knew I couldn't be around everyone else at the party anymore that night. I think I was

224

crying about Mom, about you, Lola, and about Christine.

"When we reached our house, we went down to the dock. There beneath the moon, I told him that I had to leave the Vineyard. I told him that everything had gotten too hard. That I had to leave and figure out what kind of person I could be without all the pain surrounding me all the time.

"Needless to say, he took it hard. Really hard. For years, he'd never really lost his cool throughout our on-again, off-again thing. It had always been me who'd lost it. I think he said something about how his brother had always warned him about me. He said that he'd given me everything. He said he wanted to marry me, have children, and give back to the Vineyard. He said he couldn't do it with anyone else.

"I got mad. I knew he was drunk; I knew I was even drunker. But I told him I never wanted to see him again—gosh, I can't believe I actually said that! And I threw this tiara at him. It smacked him against the head. He picked it up, and he broke it..."

At this point, Lola waved the tiara through the air. "It's not broke, Susie. It's intact."

"Look. You can tell he glued it back together," Amanda pointed out.

"Wow," Susan said. Her heart jumped into her throat. "Just wow. I never thought I'd see that thing again."

"Where do you think the clue is saying for you to go, then?" Lola asked.

"I guess the dock at our place," Susan said.

Amanda and Lola exchanged excited glances. Lola passed the tiara back to Susan and said, "I guess he wants his prom queen back, even after all these years."

225

Together, Lola, Susan, and Amanda returned to the main house. When they entered the back door, laughter and banter echoed out from the porch that overlooked the Sound. Their father, Wes, guffawed at something, then smacked his hand across his thigh.

"You can't be serious, Scott! That's incredible. You really think we should go to a Red Sox game?"

"Absolutely. Why not? A game here, a game there... you deserve it after such a chaotic summer season," Scott affirmed.

The words warmed Susan's heart. As she approached the screen door, she heard yet another sentence spring from Scott's lips.

"And you should definitely tag along, Jake. I had no idea you were such a baseball fan."

Jake? Susan's son was there? Suddenly, she burst through the screen door to discover all of them – Wes and Jake and his wife, Kristen, and the two babies, Samantha and Cody. Samantha and Cody padded around on the porch floor at Kristen's feet, wearing diapers and communicating with each other through a language all their own.

Jake and Kristen broke into grins. Wes clapped his palms together. "There she is! The woman of the hour."

Susan's eyes held on to Scott's as though they were beacons of light. She lifted the tiara into the air. Her knees were jelly.

"You want to tell me what this is?" she asked, beaming.

Scott took the tiara and placed it tenderly on her head. "It still fits you perfectly."

Susan's heart thudded. "You put all this together for me. You brought together all my favorite people in one place."

Scott shrugged. "I wanted you to know that every single part of you—your past and your present and your future—is all right by me. I want it all."

Susan's chin twitched. She felt pretty sure she was on the verge of tears. She hadn't cried in front of her children in years; it was something she'd avoided, to show them she was strong and in control.

"You still look just as good in that tiara as you did at age eighteen," he told her. "Maybe even better."

This did it. Tears flowed down her cheeks and spread out across her lips. She clenched her eyes together and laughed. Amanda rushed up behind her and wrapped her in a hug, clearly overwhelmed after never seeing her mother in such a state.

"Mom! It's okay! He did this for you! He wants you to be happy! Mom!"

Susan shook. After all the trauma of the previous year, she couldn't believe she'd gotten so lucky. She couldn't believe that Scott had decided to take her back.

When she opened her eyes again, Scott had placed his prom king crown on his head. Susan erupted into laughter.

"You kept yours too?"

He shrugged. "It's not every day you're crowned prom king. Obviously, I had to keep it around—if only to embarrass you right now in front of your kids."

Jake whistled. "I think the prom king and queen should have a first dance."

"Ha. Maybe later," Susan said, suddenly embarrassed. She winked at Scott, who turned back toward Jake and affirmed, "Yes. The day is still young."

"Is it?" Susan asked, arching her brow. "I've already gone through so many clues."

"You think I'd let you finish just after four thirty?" Scott returned. "If so, then I think you have me sorely mistaken."

Susan chuckled as Scott disappeared into the kitchen, then reappeared with cupcakes and wine for everyone.

"Before I open this box of cupcakes, you have to tell everyone the story behind them," he said conspiratorially as he placed them on the picnic table.

"You really remember everything, don't you?" Susan said with a laugh.

"Life with Susan Sheridan was never easy to forget," Scott said.

"Come on, Mom! Tell us," Jake said.

"You just want me to get it over with so you can have a cupcake," Susan teased.

"Maybe a little," Jake said.

But she could also read it in her oldest kid's eyes. He'd never seen his mother so happy and wanted to see it from all angles. He wanted to feel this other side of her. Amanda's eyes were similarly hungry.

It was as though they saw their mother as she'd always been for the first time.

"I guess it was my seventeenth birthday party," Susan began.

"She remembered. Of course, she did," Scott said, almost doubling over with laughter.

"You going to let me finish, or what?"

"Sorry."

"Anyway, Mom hired out a bigger boat for my birthday. It's at the beginning of May, but for some reason, spring was warm that year, and we all wanted to go out. Who was there? Lily, Sarah, Mom, Lola, Christine, a few other guys, and of course, Scott Frampton—my boyfriend," Susan continued. "And of course, she got these cupcakes because..."

"They were her favorites," Lola interjected. "Even I remember that. She always snuck us over there when Dad was at work."

"I had no idea," Wes said. His eyes looked far away, but his smile was serene. He clearly loved any story about Anna.

"Right. There were so many of them. She'd decorated them a lot like this. Red and white, with a big S in the center."

"I remembered almost exactly," Scott affirmed.

"So impressed with yourself, aren't you?" Susan said, chuckling. "You want to tell them what happened next, or should I?"

"In my memory, we all had a really fun time," Scott said. His eyes sparkled mischievously.

"That's not all," Susan said. She placed a hand on his chest and shoved playfully. "You wouldn't have brought these cupcakes here if you didn't remember the rest of it."

Scott's cheeks burned red. "Your mom was distracted with something. She went down to the lower deck of the boat, and the rest of us set up a quick beer pong table."

"You guys! You were such bad kids," Amanda said, clucking her tongue.

"Oh, come on, Amanda. Like you never played beer pong in high school," Susan said, casting her a look that said, *I knew exactly what you were up to the whole time.*

This shut Amanda up pretty quickly.

"Lola knew she wasn't old enough, so she kept score," Susan said. "And she was diligent about it, weren't you, Lorraine?"

Lola chuckled. "I really remember this. You and Scott

229

were up against one another. And you accused Scott of cheating..."

"The fight got pretty intense," Susan said. Her smile was so wide that she felt as though her cheeks might break.

"You accused me of stepping around the table to get closer to the cups!" Scott said. "But everyone around me was on my side. You were just a sore loser."

"I was not," Susan said.

"You really took it to a new level," Lola affirmed. "Before we knew what had happened, you'd gotten up in his face and accused him of cheating on you with that new girl, Morgan."

"Which, of course, I didn't do," Scott said.

Susan laughed. "I knew you hadn't."

"Then why did you say it?"

"I don't know. I guess I just wanted to make you mad. You got so cute when you were mad," Susan said.

"When I told you you were crazy for saying it..."

"Well, first, I shoved a cupcake into your face," Susan said with a giggle. "And then, when you wouldn't let up on me... I pushed you over the side of the boat," Susan said. She flashed a hand over her mouth and gave a half shriek.

"Mom!" Amanda cried.

"That's insane," Jake said. "I've never seen you do anything like that."

"I remember you down below swimming in the cold water," Susan said.

"It was so damn cold," Scott said.

"Everyone freaked out. One of your friends tried to jump in after you. It could have been a real mess, but you clambered up the ladder, all drenched," Susan said.

"Then your mom came upstairs and freaked out," Scott said.

Susan and Scott shared an intimate gaze. Both stirred in the memory of what had happened after that fight—when they'd climbed into Scott's truck and made love in the darkness of the night.

At the time, Susan hadn't known that her mother would be dead in only a month.

At the time, she'd just been a sweet, just-seventeen-year-old girl with her whole life ahead of her.

"Seems like you're leaving something out of the story," Lola interjected then.

Scott burst into laughter. "Maybe you're right. Maybe you're not. In any case, would anyone like a cupcake?"

The cupcakes were passed out; wine was poured. Susan sat on the porch swing next to Scott, loving the feel of his arm across her shoulders. As they ate and drank, Kristen and Jake talked about their memories as high school sweethearts.

"I guess we weren't as volatile as the two of you," Kristen said, her grin wide. "But I always felt like we were going from one fight to another."

"It kept things interesting," Jake said. "But I always knew I would find a way to marry you."

"That's funny. I thought for sure we wouldn't marry," Kristen said.

Everyone chuckled.

"Why not?" Susan asked. In her eyes, Jake and Kristen had always been the perfect couple.

Kristen tilted her head. "I don't think I knew how serious your feelings can be when you're just a kid. I think I assumed I would want to grow into a different kind of person. But in truth, I still am the person who loved yo'

And I always will be that person. And we've grown together."

The words were so perfect. Scott clutched Susan's shoulder as Jake and Kristen shared their own moment.

But the moment couldn't last for long. Suddenly, Cody stubbed his toe on the table leg, and his wail was cast out from the porch and over the Sound. Kristen whipped over, gripped him beneath the armpits, and heaved him toward her chest. She bobbed him around and cooed at him while Samantha continued to busy herself with her toy blocks below.

"Twins. I don't know how you two lived through that," Wes said with a laugh. "Having one baby at a time felt like a huge feat."

Jake, who hardly knew his grandfather at all, gave Wes a meaningful smile. "You should have seen me, Grandpa. I had these two babies strapped to my chest in this little fabric tie-thing like I was a monkey trying to tend to my young. I would go everywhere like that because I got quite a bit of time off from my engineering firm."

"Wow. Paternity leave?" Wes said, genuinely impressed. "I didn't know that was becoming a thing."

"The world is changing," Kristen said. "And I'm grateful for it. It meant that Jake and I had a say in how the babies were raised during those first months. And it's not like we had much help from Grandma." She gave Susan a well-meaning smile.

Susan laughed. "Isn't it crazy? I had a full-fledged career not even that long ago. I was building cases and interviewing criminals. It was all second nature. I never questioned it. Even Richard and I... well. Yes, he had the affair, but it's not like I was entirely unhappy."

"But you look completely different now, Mom," Jake said softly.

Susan furrowed her brow, incredulous. "What do I look like?" She couldn't imagine what her son might say next. He'd never been the sort of kid to comment on anyone's looks.

"You look like a prom queen," he said, chuckling slightly. "You look like you've just been given everything you've ever wanted."

When they'd finished eating their cupcakes, Scott admitted that the day wasn't yet finished.

"But it's time for you to say goodbye to your family for now," Scott said. "Don't worry. We'll be back to see them later tonight." He then leaned back toward them and whispered—loud enough for her to hear—"I've ordered a huge round of pizzas for seven thirty. Make sure you're hungry. That means not too many cupcakes, Lorraine."

Lola saluted him. "Ugh. Fine. If I must make space for pizza, I will."

Scott led Susan toward the dock, then around the side of the little coast, where he'd parked his boat. He helped her on it, then shifted the motor on and beamed at her as she sat beside the driver's seat.

"Where are we going?" she asked.

Scott's grin widened as he chugged out from the Vineyard and then eased west and then south toward the Aquinnah Cliffs Overlook. From the water, the cliffs were absolutely immaculate, giant. The view was different from up top, where she and Scott had gone several times as teenagers to make out.

Susan huddled closer to Scott and lifted her lips to kiss his neck tenderly. She loved the way he smelled. It was reminiscent of the old Scott, merged with this new one.

"Why did you bring me out here?" she said quietly.

Scott held her tightly. "A lot of reasons. When you first told me you wanted to leave the Vineyard, I came out here and looked out across the water for a long time. I had absolutely no idea what would happen to me next. I had no plan beyond my love for you. I knew it would be a long, dark road before I figured out what it meant to stand alone. As you've seen today, I treasured my memories with you above all things.

"But I found a way. I fought my way through those first few years, and I eventually built a business, found someone to love, and even had a son. I wouldn't trade a single moment of that time for anything."

Susan felt tears drip down her cheeks.

"I still came out here all the time," Scott continued. "And I looked out across the water and wondered if maybe, somewhere out there, you were thinking about me too. I wondered if you had ever imagined what might have been if we'd had a chance. I knew there was no way I could turn back time. But I dreamed about it up there on those cliffs."

It was the most romantic thing anyone had ever said to her. Susan felt as if she couldn't breathe.

"Do you remember that day I found you at your summer job at the restaurant, and I was crying?" Susan whispered.

Scott arched his brow. "You cried quite a bit. You were a teenage girl. You're going to have to give me a bit more context."

Susan laughed. "Fair enough. I think it was the summer I was sixteen, so 1992."

"Okay. Sure. I worked at Binkley's. The little bar and restaurant that's now closed."

"Right. And I appeared out back because I knew you would take out the garbage at some point, and I didn't want anyone to see me. I was a mess," Susan continued.

Scott furrowed his brow again. "I kind of remember it."

"I didn't tell you what had happened," Susan said. "But you held me out by the dumpsters for much longer than you were supposed to. I think you got in trouble with your boss."

"Luckily, they couldn't do anything. Nobody else wanted to be a dishwasher at Binkley's," Scott said. "But now I'm curious. What happened? Why were you crying?"

Susan laughed at the memory now. She swiped her cheeks of tears. "My period was a week late."

Scott's eyebrows jumped toward his hairline. "What?"

Susan nodded. "Yes. I was so, so anxious. I had never been late before. I'd always thought we were careful—but looking back even now, I know we weren't. Not really. I was about to make Christine sit with me in a bathroom in Edgartown as I took a test. I was terrified of the results and wanted to see you one more time before I knew about our future. As you held me, I cried because I thought I would have to find you again later that night and tell you that you were going to be a father."

All the blood had drained from Scott's cheeks. He gripped Susan as though she was his life raft. "I didn't know," he muttered. "I didn't know."

"Of course, Christine bought the test for me, and I took it, and it said I wasn't," Susan said. "It must have just been a fluke. I don't know. But for a good few days, I thought we were going to be parents. Ironically, I guess I went and got pregnant soon after leaving Oak Bluffs. And I remember thinking that the excitement wasn't the same. Richard was great at the time, and I love Jake—"

"He's a great son," Scott affirmed.

"Yes. I would never take him back. Ever," Susan continued, her voice wavering. "But I think about that pretend moment when I really thought that maybe we had made the biggest mistake of our lives. Would it really have been a mistake?"

"No. I would have loved you and our baby. I would have loved you and our baby more than the whole world and all the people in it combined." Scott breathed. He then dropped his lips over Susan's and kissed her passionately. She closed her eyes and leaned into this colossal feeling. It was more emotion than she'd known in years. It swallowed her. There was nothing left of her but heart, but love.

When their kiss broke, Susan was full-on crying. Scott swiped her tears away.

"I just want you to know that I don't want to have any more kids," she said with a laugh.

Scott joined her. "No. I don't want anyone to distract me from you. As perfect as that kid would be..."

"All those diapers," Susan said.

"Kristen looks exhausted," Scott pointed out.

"They make all their own baby food! I barely kept my kids alive!"

"Oh, whatever. I'm sure you were a perfect mother."

Susan blushed. "Okay. I tried my best. But the baby food-making thing... I was trying to get my career off the ground."

"I think they grew up just fine, despite canned baby food."

"Maybe the weirdness will come out in a few years," Susan said.

"Yeah. There's always time," Scott said.

That night, Scott and Susan returned to the big house to find piping-hot pizza, flowing wine, and beautiful, heart-warming conversation. Jake and Lola had fallen into a funny rapport, with Lola expressing that she'd hardly met any engineers in her life. "I mean, that might have saved me. All I've ever done is hang around with artists and musicians and people like that. Nobody so stable like you."

Jake laughed. "I could never have that kind of life. I guess we always heard about you growing up, Aunt Lola. How you were this bohemian, and you had this daughter, and you both lived this other kind of life..."

"Ha. That's nice," Lola said, flashing Susan a smile. "You really have to meet Audrey. She's a fantastic kid. She's in Chicago doing an internship right now."

"In what?" Jake asked.

"Journalism," Lola said proudly.

"Like her mom," Susan said.

After eating a slice of pizza, Wes crawled onto the floor with Samantha and Cody and helped them build up a little block castle. Naturally, Samantha destroyed it in only a few minutes. Wes, ever-patient in his older age, took this as a sign to build it again. The sight of Wes with his great-grandchildren was enough to overwhelm Susan.

She hadn't envisioned anything like this ever happening.

She never thought the life she'd built elsewhere

would ever unite with the one she'd had back on the Vineyard.

Yet here they were, all together.

The sun lingered over the horizon line a bit longer than normal. It seemed as though it wanted to get extra creative with the simmering oranges and pinks as it floated into the water below. As darkness crept over them, Samantha and Cody collapsed in their mother's and father's arms, and everyone's voices grew quieter so as not to wake them. Soon, Jake and Kristen sneaked upstairs to place the babies in the little cribs they'd rented for the brief trip.

"I want to build up another wing of this house." Scott breathed into Susan's ear. "It's going to be able to fit everyone you love in the world."

"Are you really so handy?" Susan asked.

"I am," Scott affirmed. "I'll fix up everything on this island until it's good enough for you to stay for good."

One by one, Lola, Amanda, and Wes retired for the night. This left only Susan and Scott on the swing, which creaked back and forth beneath them.

"What did you think of my game?" Scott asked, side-eyeing Susan.

"It was manipulative," Susan said.

"In what way?"

Susan sniffed and leaned her head against his chest. "It just reminded me of all the ways I've ever been in love with you."

"Then I guess it worked, huh?"

"I guess so."

"Now we just have to create even more memories," Scott said.

"Like this one?" Susan said.

"It's only midsummer," Scott affirmed. "And I pledge to do something memorable every single day of the year until you're sick of me."

"Be careful. You know I'll push you into the Sound," she whispered, tilting her lips up to kiss his.

"I know you will. You always keep me on my toes, Susan Sheridan. I never know what will happen next."

They kissed there on the porch swing of the Sheridan's back porch, their hearts swelling in their chests. Someday soon, Susan knew, they would have to grapple with her breast cancer diagnosis, with her father's dementia, and with the new beginnings and endings that came with lives joined together as one. But in this moment before the growing moon, she felt they could handle all of it, as long as they remained hand in hand.

Coming Next

Next in the series

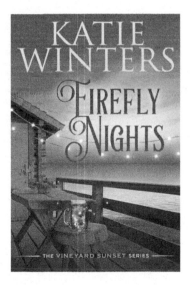

Made in United States
North Haven, CT
18 December 2023

46053344R00137